"I'm asking you to give me a chance."

Rafe's request didn't sound sincere. "You're not asking," Margaret said, "you're *demanding*. That's the way you always did things, Rafe. You haven't changed at all."

Temper flashed briefly in his eyes and was almost immediately overlaid with something far more dangerous: frustrated desire.

"How much have *you* changed, Maggie?" Rafe asked, lifting his hand to slide around the nape of her neck. "Do you still remember this?" He brushed his lips across hers in the lightest of caresses. "Do you still go all hot and trembly when I do this?" He caught her lower lip gently between his teeth and then released it.

Margaret flinched from the jolt of deep longing that knifed through her. She hadn't forgotten the effect Rafe had on her.

"Let me stay tonight," he pleaded.

"No," she answered bluntly.

He drew back slightly, releasing her. "I had a hunch you'd say that, but the standoff is over," he warned. "You're going to be mine again."

Author's Note

At the heart of every powerful romance story lies a legend. There are many romantic legends and countless modern variations on them, but they all share one thing: they are tales of brave, resourceful women who must gentle and tame the powerful, passionate men who are their true mates.

Those of us who love romance novels, readers and writers alike, understand that it is because women are willing to accept the difficult challenge of bonding with men that civilization itself continues. That, of course, explains the basic appeal of our legends.

In the Ladies and Legends trilogy, I have written three tales that are modern-day versions of three classic romantic myths. I have created *The Pirate*, *The Adventurer* and *The Cowboy*, all with heroes of mythic proportion, tamed by women who understand romance.

Jayne Ann Krentz

The Cowboy

JAYNE ANN KRENTZ

Harlequin Books

TORONTO • NEW YORK • LONDON
AMSTERDAM • PARIS • SYDNEY • HAMBURG
STOCKHOLM • ATHENS • TOKYO • MILAN

Published June 1990

ISBN 0-373-25402-4

Printed in U.S.A.

Prologue

"MARGARET, PROMISE ME you'll be careful." Sarah Fleetwood Trace, struggling to get out of her frothy wedding gown with the help of her two best friends, paused and frowned. For an instant the joyous glow that had infused her all day vanished. She looked at Margaret Lark, her fey hazel eyes clouded with sudden concern.

Margaret smiled reassuringly as she carefully lifted Sarah's veil and set it aside. "Don't worry about me, Sarah, I'll be fine. I promise to look both ways before crossing the street, count calories and not talk to strange men."

Katherine Inskip Hawthorne, concentrating on the row of tiny buttons that followed Sarah's spine, flashed a brief grin. "Don't get carried away, Margaret. You're allowed to talk to a few strange men. Just exercise some discretion."

Sarah groaned, her golden-brown hair moving in a heavy wave. Diamonds set in an old-fashioned gold design glittered in her ears. "This isn't a joke, you two. Margaret, I have a feeling..." She nibbled her lip in concentration. "I just want you to be careful for a while, all right?"

"Careful?" Margaret arched her brows in amusement. "Sarah, you know I'm always careful. What could possibly happen to me while you're on your honeymoon?"

"I don't know, that's the whole problem," Sarah said in exasperation. "I told you, I just have this feeling."

"Forget your feeling. This is your wedding day." Kate undid the last of the buttons, green eyes sparkling with laughter. "Your famous intuition probably isn't functioning normally at the moment. All the excitement, champagne and rampaging hormones have undoubtedly gotten it temporarily off track."

Margaret grinned as she hung up the wedding gown. "I don't know about Sarah's hormones, but I think it's a good bet Gideon's are rampaging. The last time I saw him, he was looking very impatient. We'd better get you changed and on your way, Sarah, before your husband comes looking for you. He's very good at finding things."

Sarah hesitated, her worried gaze still on Margaret, and then she relaxed back into the glorious smile she had worn for the past few hours. "Having a big wedding was Gideon's idea. He'll just have to put up with the necessary delays."

"Gideon doesn't strike me as the type to put up with anything he doesn't want to put up with." Margaret handed a quince-colored shirt to Sarah along with a pair of jeans.

Kate chuckled as she reached for a brush. "I had the same impression. He's a lot like Jared in that respect. Are you really going to spend your honeymoon on a treasure hunt, Sarah? I can think of better things to do."

"I can't," Sarah said blithely as she slipped into the jeans. She leaned toward the mirror to touch up her lipstick.

Margaret met her eyes in the mirror, warmed by her friend's evident happiness. "Hoping to find another treasure like the Fleetwood Flowers?"

Sarah touched the diamond earrings she was still wearing. "There will never be another treasure like the Flowers. After all, when I went looking for them, I found Gideon."

"What did you do with the other four sets of earrings?" Kate asked.

"Gideon has them safely hidden. He chose this pair for me to wear today." Sarah turned away from the mirror and buttoned the bright-colored shirt. "Okay, I'm ready." She hugged Kate and then Margaret. "Thank you both so much. I don't know what I would do without either of you. You're more important to me than I can ever say."

Margaret felt herself grow a little misty. She quickly blinked away the moisture. "You don't have to say it. We all understand."

Kate smiled tremulously. "That's right. You don't have to say it. Friends for life, right?"

"Right. Nothing will ever change that." Sarah pulled back, her expressive face full of emotion. "There's something very special about a woman's friends, isn't there?"

"Very special," Margaret agreed. She picked up Sarah's shoulder bag and handed it to her. "Something very special about a husband like Gideon Trace, too. Don't keep him waiting any longer."

Sarah's eyes danced. "Don't worry, I won't."

Margaret followed her friends into the elevator and across the hotel lobby to the large room where the wedding reception was still in full swing. A crowd composed chiefly of other writers, bookstore people and their families milled about inside, sipping champagne and dancing to the music of a small band.

As the three women stepped through the open doorway, two big, lean men moved into their path. One of them reached for Sarah's hand, a look of proud satisfaction on his face. The other flashed a wicked pirate's grin and took Kate's arm.

Margaret stood quietly to the side, studying the two males who had claimed her best friends as brides. On the surface there was no great similarity between Gideon Trace and Jared Hawthorne, other than the fact that they were both large and both moved with the kind of fluid grace that came from strength.

But although they looked nothing alike there was something about them that stamped them both as being of the same mold. They were men in the old-fashioned sense of the word—men with an inner core of steel, a bit arrogant, perhaps, a bit larger than life, but the kind of men who could be relied upon when the chips were down. They were men who lived by their own codes.

Margaret had met only one other man who was in the same league. That momentous event had occurred last year and the fallout from the explosive encounter had destroyed her career in the business world and left her bruised emotionally for a very long while. A part of her would never completely recover.

Dressed in black and white formal attire, both Jared and Gideon were devastating although neither was particularly handsome. There was an edge to them, Margaret realized—a hardness that commanded an unconscious respect.

Jared was the more outgoing of the two. He had an easy, assured manner that bordered on the sardonic. Gideon, on the other hand, had a dour, almost grim look about him that altered only when he looked at Sarah.

"About time you got down here," Gideon said to his new wife. "I've had enough wedding party to last me a lifetime."

"This was all your idea," Sarah reminded him, standing on tiptoe to brush her lips against the hard line of his jaw. "I would have been happy to run off to Las Vegas."

"I wanted to do it right," he told her. "But now it's been done right. So let's get going."

"Fine with me. When are you going to tell me where, exactly, we're going to?"

Gideon smiled faintly. "As soon as we're in the car. You've already said good-bye to your family?"

"Yes."

"Right." Gideon looked at Jared. "We're going to slide out of here. Thanks for playing best man."

"No problem." Jared held out his hand. His eyes met Gideon's in a man-to-man exchange. "See you on Amethyst Island one of these days. We'll go looking for that cache of gold coins I told you about."

Gideon nodded as he shook hands. "Sounds good. Let's go, Sarah."

"Yes, Gideon," Sarah spoke with mock demureness, her love as bright in her eyes as the diamonds in her ears. Gideon took her hand and led her swiftly out the door and into the Seattle night.

Margaret, Kate and Jared watched them go and then Kate rounded on her husband. "What cache of gold coins?"

"Didn't I ever tell you about that chest of gold my ancestor is supposed to have buried somewhere on the island?" Jared looked surprised by his own oversight.

"No, you did not."

Jared shrugged. "Must have slipped my mind. But unfortunately that old pirate didn't leave any solid clues behind so I've never bothered trying to find his treasure. Trace said he might be able to help. I took him up on the offer."

Kate smiled, pleased. "Well, at least it's a good excuse to get Gideon and Sarah out to the island soon. You'll come, too, won't you, Margaret?"

"Of course," Margaret agreed. "Wouldn't miss it for the world. Now, if you'll excuse me, I promised one more dance to a certain gentleman."

Kate's eyes widened. "You mean, an *interesting* gentleman?"

"Very interesting," Margaret said, laughing. "But unfortunately, a bit young for me." She waved at Jared's son, David, as the boy zigzagged toward them through the crowd. The youngster, who was ten years old, was an attractive miniature of his father, right down to the slashing grin. He even wore his formal clothes with the same confident ease.

"You ready to dance yet, Ms. Lark?" David asked as he came to a halt in front of her.

"I'm ready, Mr. Hawthorne."

THREE HOURS LATER, Margaret got out of the cab in front of her First Avenue apartment building and walked briskly toward the entrance. The cool Seattle summer evening closed in around her bringing with it the scent of Elliott Bay.

A middle-aged woman with a small dog bouncing at her heels came through the plate-glass doors. She smiled benignly at Margaret.

"Lovely evening, isn't it, Ms. Lark?"

"Very lovely, Mrs. Walters. Have a nice walk with Gretchen." The little dog yapped and hopped about even more energetically at the sound of her name. Margaret smiled briefly and found it something of an effort. She realized that she was suddenly feeling tired and curiously let down.

There was more to it than that, she acknowledged as she crossed the well-appointed lobby and stepped into the elevator. An unusual sense of loneliness had descended on her after the wedding reception had ended. The excitement of planning the event and the fun of seeing her two best friends again was over.

Her friends were both gone now, Sarah on her mysterious honeymoon, Kate back to Amethyst Island. It would be a long time before Margaret saw either of them again and when she did things would be a little different.

In the past they had all shared the freedom of their singlehood together. Late evening calls suggesting a stroll to the Pike Place Market for ice cream, Saturday morning coffee together at an espresso bar downtown while they bounced plot ideas off each other, the feeling of being able to telephone one another at any hour of the day or night; all that had been changed in the twinkling of two wedding rings. Sarah had found her adventurer and Kate had found her pirate.

Sarah and Kate were still her closest friends in the world, Margaret told herself. Nothing, not even marriage, could ever change that. The bond between them that had been built initially on the fact that they all wrote romance novels, had grown too strong and solid to ever be fractured by time or distance. But the practicalities of the friendship had definitely been altered.

Marriage had a way of doing that, Margaret reflected wryly. A year ago she herself had come very close to being snared in the bonds of matrimony. A part of her still wondered what her life would be like now if she had married Rafe Cassidy.

The answer to that question was easy. She would have been miserable. The only way she would have been happy with Rafe was by changing him and no woman could ever change Rafe Cassidy. Everyone who knew him recognized that Cassidy was a law unto himself.

Now what on earth had brought back the painful memories of Rafe?

She was getting maudlin. Probably a symptom of post-wedding party letdown. She thought she had successfully exorcised that damned cowboy from her mind.

Margaret stepped out of the elevator into the hushed, gray-carpeted hall. Near her door a soft light glowed from a glass fixture set above a small wooden table that held an elegant bouquet of flowers. The flowers were shades of palest mauve and pink.

Margaret halted to fish her key out of her small gilded purse. Then she slid the key into the lock and turned the handle. She thought fleetingly of bed and knew that, tired though she was, she was not yet ready to sleep. Perhaps she would go over the last chapter of her current manuscript. There were a few changes she wanted to make.

It was as she pushed open the door and stepped into the small foyer that she realized something was wrong. Margaret froze and peered into the shadows of her living room. For a moment she saw nothing but deeper shadow and then her vision adjusted to the darkness and she saw the long legs clad in gray trousers.

They ended in hand-tooled Western boots that were arrogantly propped on her coffee table. The boots were fashioned of very supple, very expensive, pearl gray leather into which had been worked an intricate design of desert flowers beautifully detailed in rich tones of gold and blue.

A pearl gray Stetson had been carelessly tossed onto the table beside the boots.

The hair on the back of Margaret's neck suddenly lifted as a sense of impending danger washed over her.

Sarah's words came back in a searing flash. *Promise me you'll be careful.*

She should have heeded her friend's intuitive warning, Margaret thought. Instinctively she took a step back toward the safety of the hall.

"Don't run from me, Maggie. This time I'll come after you."

Margaret stopped, riveted at the sound of the deep, rough-textured voice. It was a terrifyingly familiar voice—a voice that a year ago had been capable of sending chills of anticipation through her—a voice that had ultimately driven her away from the man she loved with words so cruel they still scalded her heart.

For one wild moment Margaret wondered if her thoughts had somehow managed to conjure reality out of thin air. Then again, perhaps she was hallucinating.

But the boots and the hat did not disappear when she briefly closed her eyes and reopened them.

"What on earth are you doing here?" Margaret whispered.

Rafe Cassidy's faint smile was cold in the pale gleam of the city lights that shone through the windows. "You know the answer to that, Maggie. There's only one reason I would be here, isn't there? I've come for you."

1

"HOW DID YOU GET IN HERE, Rafe?" Not the brightest of questions under the circumstances, but the only coherent one Margaret could come up with in that moment. She was so stunned, she could barely think at all.

"Your neighbor across the hall took pity on me when she found out I'd come all this way just to see you and you weren't here. It seems the two of you exchanged keys in case one of you got locked out. She let me in."

"It looks like I'd better start leaving my spare key with one of the other neighbors. Someone who has a little more common sense."

"Come on in and close the door, Maggie. We have a lot to talk about."

"You're wrong, Rafe. We have nothing to talk about." She stood where she was, refusing to leave the uncertain safety of the lighted hall.

"Are you afraid of me, Maggie?" Rafe's voice was cut glass and black velvet in the darkness. There was a soft, Southwestern drawl in it that only served to heighten the sense of danger. It was the voice of a gunfighter inviting some hapless soul to his doom in front of the saloon at high noon.

Margaret said nothing. She'd already been involved in one showdown with Rafe and she'd lost.

Rafe's smile grew slightly more menacing as he reached out and flicked on the light beside his chair. It gleamed off his dark brown hair and threw the harsh, aggressive lines of his face into stark relief. His gray, Western-cut jacket was slung over a convenient chair and his long-sleeved white shirt was open at the throat. Silver and turquoise gleamed in the elaborate buckle of the leather belt that circled his lean waist.

"There's no need to be afraid of me, Maggie. Not now."

The not so subtle taunt had the effect Margaret knew Rafe intended it to have. She moved slowly into the foyer and closed the door behind her. For an instant she was angry with herself for obeying him. Then she reminded herself that this was her apartment.

"I suppose there's not much point in telling you I don't want you here?" she asked as she tossed her small golden purse down onto a white lacquer table.

"You can kick me out later. After we've talked. Why don't you pour yourself a brandy for your nerves and we'll continue this conversation in a civilized manner."

She glanced at the glass he held in one hand and realized he'd found her Scotch. The bottle had been left over from last year. No one she knew drank Scotch except Rafe Cassidy and her father. "You were never particularly civilized."

"I've changed."

"I doubt it."

"Pour the brandy, Maggie, love," he advised a little too gently.

She thought about refusing and knew it wouldn't do much good. Short of calling the police there was no way to get Rafe out of her apartment until he was ready to leave. Pouring brandy would at least give her something to do with her hands. Perhaps the liquor would stop the tiny shivers that seemed to be coursing through her.

Rafe's hard mouth twisted with faint satisfaction as he realized she was going to follow orders. With laconic grace he took his booted feet off the coffee table, got up and followed her into the gray and white kitchen.

"I never did like this picture," he said idly as he passed the framed painting on the wall. "Always looked like recycled junk stuck in paint to me."

"Our taste in art was one of several areas in which we had no common ground, wasn't it, Rafe?"

"Oh, we had a lot in common, Maggie. Especially in the middle of the night." He stood lounging in the doorway as she rummaged in the cupboard for a glass. She could feel his golden-brown eyes on her, the eyes that had always made her think of one of the larger species of hunting cat.

"Then again, the middle of the night was about the only time you had available to devote to our relationship," she reminded him bitterly. "And I recall a lot of nights when I didn't even get that much time. There were plenty of nights when I awoke and discovered you were out in the living room going through more papers, working on more ways to take some poor unsuspecting company by surprise."

"So maybe I worked a little too much in those days."

"That's putting it mildly, Rafe. You're obsessed with Cassidy and Company. A mere woman never stood a chance of competing."

"Things are different now. You look good, Maggie. Real good."

Her hand shook a little at the controlled hunger in his voice. The brandy bottle clinked awkwardly on the rim of the glass. "You look very much the same, Rafe." *Overwhelming, fierce, dangerous. Still a cowboy.*

He shrugged. "It's only been a little over a year."

"Not nearly long enough."

"You're wrong. It's been too damn long. But we'll get to that in a minute." He picked up her brandy glass as soon as she finished pouring and handed it to her with mock gallantry. His big hand brushed against her fingers in a deliberate movement designed to force physical contact.

Margaret snatched her glass out of his hand and turned her back on him. She led the way into the living room. Beyond the wide expanse of windows the lights of Seattle glimmered in the night. Normally she found the view relaxing but tonight it offered no comfort.

She sat down in one of the white leather chairs. It was something of a relief not to have to support her own weight any longer. She felt weak. "Don't play games with me, Rafe. You played enough of them a year ago. Just say whatever it is you feel you have to say and then get out."

Rafe's eyes raked her face as he sat down across from her. He gave her his thin smile. It was the only sort of smile he had. "Let's not get into the subject of who was playing games a year ago. It's a matter of opinion."

"Not *opinion*. Fact. And as far as I'm concerned, the facts are very clear."

He shook his head, refusing to be drawn. "We can sort it all out some other time, if ever. Personally, I think it's best to just forget most of what happened a year ago."

"Easy for you to say. It wasn't your career and your professional reputation that were ruined."

Rafe's eyes darkened. "You could have weathered the storm. You chose to walk away from your career and take up writing full-time."

Margaret allowed herself a small, negligent shrug. "You may be right. As it happens I had a better career to walk to. Best professional move I could have made. I love my writing and I can assure you I don't miss the business jungle one bit. I wouldn't go back for anything." Her writing, which had been part-time until last year, had become full-time after the disaster and she didn't regret it for a moment.

"You dropped out of sight. Found a new apartment. Took your listing out of the phone book." Rafe leaned back in his chair and crossed his ankles once more on the coffee table. He sipped reflectively at his Scotch. "Took me a while to find you when I started looking. Your publisher refused to give out your address and your father was not what you'd call cooperative."

"I should hope not. I told him I never wanted to see you again as long as I lived. I assumed the feeling was mutual."

"It was. For a while."

"When did you start looking for me?"

"A few months ago."

"Why?" she demanded bluntly.

"I thought I made that clear. I want you back."

Her stomach tightened and her pulse thrummed as it went into a primitive fight-or-flight rhythm. "No. Never. You don't want me, Rafe. You never wanted me. You just used me."

His fingers clenched the glass but his face betrayed no change of expression. "That's a lie, Maggie, love. Our relationship had nothing to do with what happened between Cassidy and Company and Moorcroft's firm."

"The hell it didn't. You used me to get inside information. Worse, you wanted to taunt Jack Moorcroft with the news that you were sleeping with his trusted manager, didn't you? Don't bother to deny it, Rafe, because we both know it's the truth. You told me so yourself, remember?"

Rafe's jaw tightened. "I was mad as hell that morning when I found you warning Moorcroft about my plans. As far as I was concerned, you'd betrayed me."

The injustice of that seared her soul. "I worked for Jack Moorcroft and I discovered you were after the company he was trying to buy out; that you'd used me to help you try to outmaneuver him. What did you expect me to do?"

"I expected you to stay out of it. It had nothing to do with you."

"I was just your pawn in the game, is that it? Did you think I'd be content with that kind of role?"

Rafe drew a deep breath, obviously fighting for his self-control. "I've thought about it a lot during the past year. Every damn day, as a matter of fact, although I told myself at the time that I wasn't going to waste a minute looking for excuses for you. It took me months to calm down enough to start assessing the mess from your point of view."

"Since when did you ever bother to examine anything from my point of view?"

"Take it easy, Maggie, love. I realize now that you felt you had some legitimate reason to do what you did. Yes, sir, I've given it a lot of thought and the way I see it, the whole thing was basically a problem of confused loyalties. You were mixed up, that's all." His mouth curved ruefully. "And a multimillion-dollar deal went down the drain because of it, but I'm willing to let bygones be bygones."

"Oh, gee, thanks. Very magnanimous of you. Rafe, let's get one thing straight. I never asked you to make excuses for me. I don't want you making excuses for me. I don't need your forgiveness because I didn't do anything wrong."

"I'm trying to explain that I don't feel the same way about what happened as I did last year," he said, his voice edged with impatience.

"If you're feeling a twinge or two of guilt about the way you used me and the way you treated me afterward, I hereby absolve you. Believe me, if I were in the same situation again, I'd act exactly the same way. I'd still warn Moorcroft. There. Does that make you feel justified in treating me the way you did?"

He stared at her, his leonine eyes brilliant with some undefined emotion. "You weren't his mistress, were you? Not before or afterward."

She wanted to strike him. It took everything she had to maintain her self-control. "Why should I confirm or deny that?"

"Moorecroft said you'd been sleeping with him up until he realized I was interested in you. He saw a golden opportunity and decided to take advantage of it. He told you to go to me, let me seduce you, see what you could learn."

Margaret shuddered. "You and Moorcroft are both outright bastards."

"He lied to me that morning, didn't he? You were never his."

"I was never any man's."

"You were mine for a while." Rafe took another swallow of his Scotch. "And you're going to be mine again."

"Not a chance. Never in a million years. Not if you were the last man on earth."

Rafe ignored each carefully enunciated word. He frowned thoughtfully as he stared into the darkness. "From what I can tell, you never even saw Moorcroft again after you handed in your resignation. Why was that, Maggie? Did he kick you out because you'd become a liability? Was that it? He didn't want you working for him once the scandal broke? Did he force you to resign?"

"Wouldn't you have asked for my resignation in the same circumstances? If you found out one of your top management people was sleeping with your chief competitor, wouldn't you have demanded she leave?"

"Hell, yes. Everyone who works for me knows that in exchange for a paycheck the one thing I demand is loyalty."

Margaret sighed. "Well, at least you're honest about it. As it happens, Jack didn't have to ask me to turn in my resignation. I was very anxious to go by then. I'd been planning to quit my job in another couple of years to pursue my writing full-time, anyway. The scandal last year just speeded up the process a bit."

Rafe swore softly. "I didn't come here to argue with you. I've told you, as far as I'm concerned, the past is behind us and it's going to stay there."

"Why did you come here? You still haven't made your reasons clear. I'm out of the business world these days, Rafe. I have no secrets to spill that might help you force some company into an unwilling merger or enable you to buy out some poor firm that's gotten itself into a financial mess. I can't help you in any way."

"Stop making it sound as if I only used you for inside information," Rafe said through gritted teeth.

"You knew who I was before you approached me at that charity function where we met, didn't you?"

"So what? That doesn't mean I plotted to use you."

"Oh, come on, now, Rafe. I'm not a complete fool. Do you swear it never crossed your mind that it might be useful to talk to someone who was as close to Jack Moorcroft as I was? Wasn't that why you introduced yourself in the first place?"

"What the hell does it matter why I approached you that first time? Within five minutes of meeting you I knew that what we were going to have together had nothing to do with business. I asked you to marry me, damn it."

She nearly choked on her brandy. "Yes, you did, didn't you? The first week I met you. And I was actually considering it even though every instinct I possessed was screaming at me to run." That was not quite the truth. A few of her more primitive instincts had shouted at her to stay and take the risk.

"I'm going to ask you again, Maggie."

She was suddenly so light-headed she thought she might faint. "What did you say?"

"You heard me." Rafe got to his feet and paced soundlessly across the white carpet to the window. He stood looking out into the night. "I'm prepared to give you a little time to get accustomed to the notion again. I know this is coming out of the blue for you. But I want you, Maggie. I've never stopped wanting you."

"Is that right? I distinctly recall you telling me you never wanted to see me again."

"I lied. To myself and to you."

She shook her head in disbelief. "I saw the rage in you that morning. You hated me."

"No. Never that. But I was in a rage. I admit it. I couldn't believe you'd gone straight to Moorcroft to warn him about my plans. When you didn't even bother to defend yourself, I decided I'd been had. Moorcroft was more than willing to reinforce the idea."

"I did go straight to Moorcroft," Margaret agreed grimly. "But I was the one who'd been had. As far as I'm concerned you and Moorcroft both took advantage of me. It's one of the reasons I left the business world, Rafe. I realized I didn't have the guts for it. I couldn't handle the level of warfare. It made me sick."

"You were too soft for that world, Maggie, love. I knew that from the first day I met you. If you'd married me, you would have been out of it."

"Let's be honest with each other, Rafe. If I'd married you a year ago, we'd have been divorced by now."

"No."

"It's the truth, whether you want to admit it or not. I couldn't have tolerated your idea of marriage for long. I knew that at the time. That's why I put off giving you my answer during those two months we were together." She also knew that if the blow-up hadn't occurred, she probably would have succumbed to Rafe's pressure tactics and married him. She would have found a proposal from Rafe impossible to resist. She had been in love with him.

Rafe glanced over his shoulder, his mouth gentling. "It might have been a little rough at times but it would have worked. I'd have made it work. This time it will work."

Margaret squeezed her eyes shut on hot tears. Determinedly she blinked them back. When she looked at Rafe again, she saw him through a damp mist but she was fairly certain she wouldn't actually break down and cry. She must not do that. This man homed in on weakness the way a predator homed in on prey.

"I'm surprised at you, Rafe. If you felt this strongly about the matter, why did you wait an entire year to come after me?" Margaret thought with fleeting anguish of the months she had spent hoping he would do just that before she had finally accepted reality and gotten on with her life. "It's not like you to be so slow about going after what you want."

"I know. But in this case things were different." His shoulders moved in an uneasy, uncharacteristic gesture. "I'd never been in a situation like that before." He turned toward her and swirled the Scotch in his glass. His eyes were thoughtful when he finally raised them to meet hers. "For the first few months I couldn't even think clearly. I was a menace to everyone during the day and stayed up most of the nights trying to work myself into a state of exhaustion so I could get a couple of hours' sleep. Ask Hatcher or my mother if you want to know what I was like during that period. They all refer to it as the Dark Ages."

"I can imagine you were a little upset at having your business plans ruined," Margaret said ironically. "There was a lot of money on the line and Moorcroft's firm cleaned up thanks to my advance warning. You lost that time around and we all know how you feel about losing."

Rafe's gaze sparked dangerously but the flare of anger was quickly dampened. "I can handle losing. It happens. Occasionally. But I couldn't handle the fact that you'd turned traitor and I couldn't deal with the way you'd walked out without a backward glance."

"What did you expect me to do after you told me to get out of your sight?"

Rafe smiled bleakly. "I know. You were hardly the type to cry and tell me you were sorry or to grovel on your knees and beg me to forgive you and take you back, were you?"

"Not bloody likely," Margaret muttered. "Not when I was the innocent victim in that mess."

"I used to fantasize about it, you know."

"Fantasize about what? Me pleading for your forgiveness?"

He nodded. "I was going to let you suffer for a while; let you show me how truly sorry you were for what you'd done and then I was going to be real generous and take you back."

"On your terms, of course."

"Naturally."

"It's a good thing you didn't hold your breath, isn't it?"

"Yeah, I'd have passed out real quick because you sure as hell never came running back to me. At first I assumed that was because you'd gone back to your affair with Moorcroft."

"Damn you, there never was any affair with Moorcroft."

"I know, I know." He held up a hand to cut off her angry protest. "But I couldn't be certain at the time and I could hardly call up Moorcroft and ask, could I? He'd have laughed himself sick."

"It would have served you right."

"My pride was already in shreds. I wasn't about to let Jack Moorcroft stomp all over it."

"Of course not. Your pride had been a lot more important than whatever it was we had together, hadn't it?"

He turned to face her. "I'm here tonight, aren't I? Doesn't that say something about my priorities?"

She eyed him warily. "It says you're up to something. That's all it says. And I don't want any part of it. I learned my lesson a year ago, Rafe. Only a fool gets burned twice."

"Give me a chance to win you back, Maggie. That's all I'm asking."

"No," she said, not even pausing to think about her response. There was only one safe answer.

He watched her for a moment and Margaret didn't like the look in his eyes. She'd seen it before and she knew what it meant. Rafe was running through his options, picking and choosing his weapons, analyzing the best way to stage his next assault. When he moved casually back to the white chair and sat down, Margaret instinctively tensed.

"You really are afraid of me, aren't you, Maggie, love?"

"Yes," she admitted starkly. "You can be an extremely ruthless man and I don't know what you've got up your sleeve."

"Well, it's true there are a few things you don't know yet," Rafe said softly.

"I don't want to know them."

"You will."

"All I want is for you to leave."

"I told you when you opened the door tonight that you don't have to be afraid of me."

"I'm not afraid of you. But I have some common sense and I will admit I'm extremely cautious around you. I definitely do not intend to get involved with you again, Rafe."

He turned the glass in his hands. "What I had in mind was a little vacation for you."

That alarmed her. "A *vacation*? I don't need or want a vacation."

"At the ranch," he continued, just as if she hadn't spoken.

"Your ranch in Arizona?"

"You never had a chance to see it. You'll like it, Maggie."

"No, absolutely not. I don't want to go to any ranch. I hate ranches. If I wanted to go on a vacation, I'd choose a luxury resort on a South Sea island, not a ranch."

"You'll like this one." Rafe swallowed the last of the Scotch. "It's just outside of Tucson. I grew up there. Inherited it when Dad died."

"No."

"You don't have to worry," Rafe said gently. "You won't be alone with me. My mother will be there."

"I thought she lived in Scottsdale."

"She does. But she's paying me a visit. My sister, Julie, is going to drop in on us, too. She lives in Tucson, you know. I thought you'd feel more comfortable about going down there if you knew you weren't going to be completely alone with me."

"Look, I don't care who's going to be down there. Rafe, stop stalking me like this. I mean it."

"There'll be someone else there, too, honey."

"I just told you, I don't care who's there. In case you didn't realize it, knowing your mother will be around is not much of an incentive for me to go to Tucson. She undoubtedly hates my guts. She thinks the sun rises and sets on you. She made her opinion of me clear that one time I met her last year and I'm sure she thinks even less of me after what happened between us. I'm sure she blames me for your losing Spencer Homes to Moorcroft. I wouldn't be surprised if your sister feels exactly the same."

"Now, Maggie, love, you've got to allow for the fact that people change. My mother is looking forward to seeing you again."

"I don't believe that for a minute and even if it's true, I'm not particularly anxious to see her."

"You'd better get used to the idea of seeing her," Rafe said. "She's going to marry your father."

"She's *what*?" Margaret felt as if the world had just fallen away beneath her feet. She clutched at her brandy glass.

"You heard me."

"I don't believe you. You're lying. My father would have said something."

"He hasn't said anything because I asked him not to. I wanted to handle this my own way. He's the other person who will be at the ranch while you're there, by the way."

"Oh, my God." She felt physically sick as she put the untouched brandy down on the table.

"Are you all right?" Rafe frowned in concern.

"No."

"It's not as bad as all that. They make a great couple, as a matter of fact."

"When . . . where . . . how did they meet?"

"I introduced them about four months ago."

"For God's sake, why?"

"Because I had a hunch they'd hit it off. Your father wasn't too keen on the idea at first, I'll admit. He was more inclined to string me up from the nearest tree. Seems he was under the impression I was the bad guy in that mess last year. When I straightened him out on a few details, including the fact that I still wanted to marry you, he settled down and saw the light of sweet reason. Then he met Mom and fell like a ton of bricks."

Margaret stared at Rafe in bewildered horror. "I don't understand any of this. What's behind it? You never do anything unless the bottom line is worth it. *What is going on here?*"

He smiled his thin smile. "If you want to find out you'll have to take a couple of weeks off and come down to the ranch." He reached inside the jacket he'd slung over the back of the chair and removed an airline ticket folder. "I've made the reservations for you. You're scheduled on the eight o'clock flight to Tucson next Monday."

"You're out of your mind if you think you can just walk in here and take control of my life like this. I'm not going anywhere."

"Suit yourself, but I think you'll want to find out what's happening and the only way to do it is to come down to Arizona."

"If my father is crazy enough to get involved with your mother, that's his affair. I'll give him my opinion when he asks for it, but until then, I'm staying out of it."

"It isn't just their relationship that's at stake," Rafe said calmly.

Margaret dug her fuchsia-colored nails into the white leather upholstery. "I knew it," she bit out. "With you there's always a business reason. Tell me the rest, damn you."

"Well, it's true your father and I are thinking of doing a little business together."

"Good Lord. What kind of business?"

"I'm going to buy Lark Engineering."

It was the final bombshell as far as Margaret was concerned. She leaped to her feet. She wanted to call him a liar again, but even as the words crossed her mind, she was terribly, coldly afraid. "My father would never sell the firm to you. He built it from the ground up. It's his whole life. If he's thinking of selling out, it's because you're forcing his hand. What have you done, Rafe? What kind of leverage are you using against him?"

Rafe rose slowly to his feet, looming over her. He dominated the elegant room—a dark, dangerous intruder who threatened Margaret's hard-won peace of mind as nothing else ever had. She looked up at him, feeling small and very vulnerable. But she refused to step back out of reach. She would not give him the satisfaction.

"You really don't think very much of me, do you?" Rafe's mouth was taut with his rigidly controlled anger. "It's a good thing I learned something about handling my own pride this past year because the look in your eyes right now is enough to make a man feel about two inches tall."

"Really?" Her voice was scathing. "And do you feel two inches tall?"

"No, ma'am," he admitted. "But I probably would if I were guilty of whatever it is you think I'm doing to your father. Lucky for me I'm as innocent as a new foal."

"Are you saying you're not forcing him to sell out to you?"

"Nope. Ask him."

"I will, damn you."

"You'll have to come down to the ranch to do that," Rafe said. "Because that's where he is and he won't re-assure you on the phone."

"Why not?"

"Because he knows I want some time with you down there and he's agreed to act as the bait. You'll have to fly to Arizona if you want to convince yourself that I'm not pulling a fast one."

"And if I don't go?"

"Then I reckon you'll sit here in Seattle and worry a lot."

She shook her head, dazed. "I don't believe any of this. Why are you doing it?"

"I've told you why I'm doing it. I want another chance with you. This is the only way I know to get it."

"Even if that disaster last year didn't stand between us, we have no business thinking about getting involved again. I've told you that. I could never marry you, Rafe. Not for long, at any rate."

"I'll make you change your mind."

"Impossible. I know you too well now. The truth is, I knew you too well last year. That's the reason I didn't give you an answer the first time you asked. Or the second or the third. Your first love is business and your overriding passion in life is for making money, not making love."

Rafe contrived to look hurt. "I don't recall you complaining too loud in bed."

Margaret clenched her fists. "On the rare occasions you managed to find time to take me to bed you performed just fine."

"Why, thank you, honey. It's real sweet of you to remember."

"You're missing the point," she hissed.

"Yeah?"

"The point is, you don't have a lot of time in your life for a relationship of any kind. During the two months we were dating you were always flying into Seattle for a weekend and then flying out again Monday morning. Or you would show up on my doorstep at midnight on a Wednesday, take me to bed and then disappear at six the next day to get to a business conference in L.A."

"I admit I used to do a fair amount of traveling, but I've cut back lately."

"And when you weren't traveling, you were tied up at the office. Remember all those times you called from Tucson and told me you wouldn't be able to make it up here to Seattle? I was expected to rearrange all my plans to accommodate you. Or else you'd arrive with a briefcase full of work and Doug Hatcher in tow and the two of you would take over my living room for a full day."

"Now, honey, there was a lot going on at the time."

"With you there always will be a lot going on. It's your nature. Your mother was kind enough to point that out to me. Said you were just like your father. You thrive on your work. Beating the competition to the draw is the most important thing in your life."

"You're getting carried away now, Maggie, love. Just take it easy, honey. I'm dead serious about this. I want to get married."

"Oh, I believe you. You'd find a wife useful. You want a wife who will be a convenience for you—someone to handle your entertaining, your home, your social life. Someone who will warm your bed when you want it warmed and stay out of your way when you've got other things to do. Someone who knows how to live in your world and who will accommodate her entire life to yours. In short, you want the perfect corporate wife."

"Give me the next couple of weeks to prove that I'm willing to make a few accommodations of my own."

Margaret's head came up sharply. "You're hardly starting out on a promising foot, are you? You're trying to blackmail me into going down to your ranch."

He sighed. "Only because I know it's a sure-fire way to get you there. Maggie, listen to me . . ."

She glared at him. "Don't call me Maggie. I never did like the way you called me that. No one else ever calls me Maggie."

Rafe's brows rose. "Your dad does."

"That changes nothing. I dislike being called Maggie."

"You never said anything about it before."

"It didn't seem worth arguing about last year. Good grief, there wasn't time to argue about it. This year is different, however. I'm not putting up with anything from you this year."

"I see. That's too bad. I always kind'a liked Maggie."

"I don't."

"All right," he said soothingly, "I'll try to remember to call you Margaret."

"You don't have to try to remember anything. You won't be around long enough to make the mistake very often."

"You're not going to give an inch, are you?"

"No." Margaret eyed him defiantly.

Rafe's mouth curved faintly. "I had a feeling you were going to be like that. Which is why I went to so much effort to set this whole thing up the way I did. I need you to give me a chance to prove that I've changed. I'm only asking for two weeks."

"You're not asking, you're demanding. That's the way you always did things, Rafe. You haven't changed at all."

Temper flashed briefly in his eyes and was almost immediately overlaid with something far more dangerous: frustrated desire. Rafe lifted a hand to slide around the nape of Margaret's neck beneath the neat chignon of her hair. She froze.

"How much have you changed, Maggie?" he asked softly, his mouth only inches from hers. "Do you still remember this?" He brushed his lips across hers in the lightest of caresses. "Do you still go all hot and trembly when I do this?" He caught her lower lip gently between his teeth and then released it.

Margaret flinched from the jolt of deep longing that knifed through her. She did not move. She was not sure she could have moved if she'd tried. She was paralyzed—a rabbit confronted by a mountain lion.

Rafe's mouth slanted across hers again and she was thoroughly confused by the unexpected tenderness of his kiss. His fingers stroked her nape, feather-light against her sensitive skin. A tremor sizzled along her nerve endings. She shivered.

"Yeah, you still do, don't you? I've been thinking about this for the past year," Rafe muttered. "One whole year, damn you. Every night and every day. There were times when I thought I'd go clear out of my mind with wanting you. How could you do that to me, Maggie?"

She was shaken by the bleak depths in his voice. "If it was the sex you missed, I'm sure there must have been someone around to give you what you wanted."

"No," he stated harshly. "There was no one. There hasn't been anyone since you, Maggie."

She stared up at him in shock. When he finally had found time for bed, Rafe had proved himself to be a deeply sensual man. She remembered that much quite vividly. "I don't believe you."

"Believe it," he growled as his mouth grazed hers one more time. "God knows I do. I had to live through every night alone and it nearly drove me crazy."

"Rafe, you can't walk back in here after a whole year and do this to me," Margaret said desperately. "I won't let you."

"Let me stay tonight."

"No."

He drew back slightly, releasing her. "I had a hunch you'd say that but I had to ask. Don't worry about it, I've waited this long, I can wait a little longer."

"You'll wait until hell freezes over," she said crisply. "You've said what you had to say, Rafe. Now leave."

He hesitated briefly. Then he nodded and picked up his hat. He jammed it down low over his glittering eyes.

As he reached for his jacket, he glanced at the airline ticket he'd left on the table. "Next Monday. The eight o'clock flight."

"I won't be on it."

"Please."

Margaret's mouth fell open in amazement. "What did you say?"

"I said *please*. Please be on the eight o'clock flight. Come to Arizona to talk to the woman who will probably be marrying your father. Come to Arizona to find out what kind of evil deal I've cooked up to get your dad to sell his company to me. Come to Arizona to see if I really have changed. Come to Arizona to give us both a second chance."

"I'd be a fool to do it."

"There hasn't been anyone else for either of us for the past year, Maggie. That should tell us both something." He hooked the jacket over his shoulder and strode to the door.

"Rafe, wait, I'm not going to do it, do you hear me? I won't be on that plane." Margaret managed to unstick herself from the carpet and go after him, but she was too late.

The door closed softly behind him before she could ask him how he knew there had been no one else for her during the past year.

2

IT HAD BEEN THE LONGEST YEAR of his life, Rafe thought savagely, and Maggie looked as if she'd spent it sleeping on rose petals and sipping tea. It was almost more than he could take to see her looking so serene and untouched by the past twelve months.

He clung to the knowledge that she had been as celibate as he had. It was the only thing that gave him any real hope. On some level she had been waiting for him, he told himself. On some level she was still his and knew it.

Outside on the street in front of her apartment building he managed to find a cab for the ride back to his hotel. Knowing he was heading toward a lonely hotel room when he should have been spending the night in Maggie's bed did nothing for Rafe's temper. Still, the players in the game were finally in position at last and the first moves had all been made. The action was ready to start.

She was as striking as ever, he admitted to himself as he sprawled back against the seat in the cab. More so. She was a little more sure of herself now than she had been a year ago. *And a hell of a lot less willing to accommodate herself to his schedule*, he thought with grim humor.

The sight of her tonight had nearly shattered his carefully honed self-control. He had promised himself he would remain in command of the situation, but when she had walked through the door his first instinct had been to pull her down onto the carpet of her elegant living room and make love to her until she was wild. He needed desperately to feel her respond to him the way she had the last time on that memorable night before everything had gone up in smoke. Lord, he was starving for her.

He had never been so hungry in his life and he had to be patient. He stared moodily at the cheerfully garish lights of the public market as the cab driver turned east on Pike Street. It had been a year since he had seen Seattle at night.

The cab halted in front of the lobby of the expensive hotel and Rafe got out. He reached for his wallet.

"Nice boots," the cabbie remarked as he pocketed the excessive tip.

"Thanks." Rafe turned toward the lobby.

"Hey, if you've got nothin' else to do this evenin'," the cabbie called after him, "I can give you a couple of suggestions. I know where the action is here in town. No sense spendin' the night alone."

"Why not? It's the way I spend all of my nights lately."

Rafe went on into the marble and wood-paneled lobby. He couldn't stop picturing Maggie as she had looked tonight standing framed in the doorway of her apartment. Her sleek black hair had been pulled back to accent the delicate lines of her face. Her aquamarine eyes were even larger and more compelling than they had been in his dreams.

The sophisticated silk dress she wore glided over subtle, alluring curves. She looked as if she'd put on a couple of pounds but they had gone to the right places. She still moved with the grace of a queen.

Maggie had obviously found her footing in her new career as a writer. In fact, she looked depressingly content. Rafe felt like chewing nails. It seemed only fair that she should have suffered as much as he had. But apparently she hadn't.

He reminded himself once more of the report from the discreet investigative agency he had employed. Maggie dated only rarely and never seriously. Until recently she had spent a lot of her free time with two other women who had been friends of hers for the past couple of years.

Rafe had never met Sarah Fleetwood and Katherine Inskip but their names showed up so often in the reports that he had come to think of the unknown women as duennas for his lady. Somewhere along the line he had unconsciously started depending on them to keep Maggie out of trouble.

Trouble meant another man in Maggie's life, as far as Rafe was concerned. But as luck would have it, Sarah and Katherine had been the ones who had found the other men. He wasn't making his move any too soon, Rafe told himself. No sense leaving a woman like Maggie at loose ends for very long.

Rafe went into the hotel bar and found a secluded booth. He ordered a Scotch and sat brooding over it, analyzing the scene in Maggie's living room, searching for flaws in the way he'd handled the delicate negotiations, wondering if he'd applied just the right amount of pressure.

He'd spent months putting the plan together and he'd used every lever he could find. He would have bargained with the devil himself to get Maggie back. But tonight he'd played the last cards in his hand. Now he could only pray Maggie would be on that Monday morning flight to Tucson. His whole future was hanging in the balance and Rafe knew it. The knowledge made his insides grow cold.

THE BOOK SIGNING SESSION on Saturday morning went well. Margaret thoroughly enjoyed talking to the readers and other writers in the area who had made their way by car, bus and monorail into downtown Seattle to meet the author of *Ruthless*. She was especially grateful for the enthusiastic crowd this morning because it took her mind off the difficult decision that had to be made by Monday. For a while, at least, she did not have to think about Rafe Cassidy.

"I just loved *Ruthless*." A happily pregnant woman with a toddler clinging to her skirts handed her copy of the book to Margaret to sign. "I always feel good after I've read one of your books. I really love your heroes. They're great. Oh, Christine is the name, by the way."

"Thanks, Christine. I'm glad you liked the book. I appreciate your coming downtown today." Margaret wrote Christine's name on the title page, a brief message and then signed her own name with a flourish.

"No problem. Wouldn't have missed it for the world. I was an account executive at a brokerage house here in Seattle before I quit to raise kids for a while. I really identify with the business settings in your stories. When's your next book due out?"

"In about six months."

"Can't wait. Another hero like Roarke, I hope?"

Margaret smiled. "Of course." Roarke was the name of the hero in *Ruthless*, but the truth was all her heroes were similar. They all bore a striking resemblance to Rafe Cassidy. That had been true from her first book, which had been written long before she had ever met Rafe. It was probably why she had fallen so hard and so fast for him when he'd exploded into her life last year, she thought.

At first sight she had been certain Rafe was the man of her dreams.

Except for the boots, of course. Looking back on the disaster Margaret knew she ought to have been warned when her dream man showed up in a Stetson, fancy boots and a silver belt buckle. In her books her heroes always wore European-styled suits and Italian leather shoes.

Hard, savvy and successful businessmen for the most part, her male characters always had a ruthless edge that made them a real challenge for the heroines. But in the end, unlike Rafe, they all succumbed to love.

A stylish-looking woman in a crisp suit who was standing directly behind Christine extended her copy of *Ruthless*. "Christine's right. Give us another hero like Roarke. He was great. I love the tough-guy-who-can-be-taught-to-love type. I think of them as cowboys in business suits."

Margaret stared at her. "Cowboys? Good heavens, what makes you call them that? I like the sophisticated urban type. That's the kind I always write about."

The woman shook her head with a knowing look in her eye. "But your heroes are all cowboys in disguise, didn't you know that?"

Margaret eyed her thoughtfully. She had long ago learned to appreciate some of the insights her readers had into her books but this one took her back. "You really think so?"

"Trust me. I know cowboys when I see them, even if they are wearing two hundred dollar silk shirts."

"She's right, you know," another woman in line announced with a grin. "When I'm reading one of your books, I always visualize a cowboy."

"What on earth makes you do that?" Margaret asked in utter amazement.

The woman paused, considering her answer. "I think it's got something to do with their basic philosophies of life—the way they think and act. They've got a lot of old-fashioned attitudes about women and honor and that kind of thing. The sort of attitudes we all associate with the Old West."

"It's true," someone else in line agreed. "The shootouts take place in corporate boardrooms instead of in front of the saloon, but the feeling is the same." She leaned forward to extend her copy of *Ruthless*. "The name is Rachel."

"Rachel." Margaret hurriedly signed the book and handed it back. "Thank you."

"Thank you." Rachel winked mischievously. "Speaking of cowboys," she said, exchanging a smile with the other woman, "maybe one of these days you can give us the real thing, horse and all."

"We'll look forward to it," the first woman declared as she collected her signed book.

Margaret managed a laugh and shook her head, feeling slightly dazed. "We'll see," she temporized, not wanting to offend the readers by telling them she'd once run into a real corporate gunslinger who was very much a cowboy and the result had been something other than a happy ending.

She turned, smiling, to greet the next person in line and nearly dropped her pen when she caught sight of the familiar figure standing in front of her. It never rained but it poured, she thought ironically.

"Hello, Jack. What are you doing here? I didn't know you read romance."

Jack Moorcroft smiled down at her, his light hazel eyes full of genuine curiosity. "So you really made it work, did you?"

"Made what work? My writing? Yes, I've been fortunate."

"I didn't think you could turn it into a full-fledged career."

"Neither did anyone else."

"Can I buy you a coffee or a drink when you're finished here? I'd like to talk to you."

"Let me guess what this is all about. I haven't seen you since the day I resigned. You moved the headquarters of Moorcroft Industries to San Diego nearly a year ago, according to the papers. And now, out of a clear blue sky you suddenly show up again in Seattle two days after Rafe Cassidy magically reappears. Can I assume there's a connection or is this one of those incredible coincidences that makes life so interesting?"

"You always were one smart lady. That's why I hired you in the first place."

"Forget the flattery, Jack. I'm immune."

"I get the feeling you're not enjoying old ties with your former business associates?"

"You're very perceptive for a businessman."

Jack nodded, accepting the rebuff. "I think I can understand. You got a little mauled there at the end, didn't you? Cassidy can play rough. But I do have to talk to you. It's important, Margaret. Coffee? For old times' sake?"

She sighed, wishing she could think of a polite way out of the invitation. But the truth was Jack had been a reasonably good boss. And he'd never actually asked for her resignation. It had been her idea to leave the firm. "All right. Coffee. I'll be finished here in another fifteen minutes or so."

"I'll wait."

Twenty minutes later Margaret bid goodbye to the bookstore manager and the last of the readers who had dropped by the store to say hello. Slinging her stylish leather shoulder bag over her arm, she went to join Jack Moorcroft who was waiting patiently at the entrance of the store near the magazine racks.

He smiled when he saw her and put back the copy of *Forbes* he had been perusing. She studied him objectively as he held the door for her. Moorcroft was five years older than Rafe, which made him forty-three. On the surface he fit her mental image of a hero better than Rafe ever did. For one thing, there wasn't a trace of the cowboy in Moorcroft's attire or his accent. He was pure corporate polish.

Moorcroft was also a genuinely good-looking man. He kept himself trim by daily workouts at an exclusive health club and he dressed with impeccable finesse. His light brown hair was streaked with silver and thinning a bit, but that only served to give him a distinguished look. His suit was European in cut and the tie was silk.

By right Moorcroft should have been a living, breathing replica of one of her heroes but Margaret had never once thought of him that way.

In addition to his beautifully cut suits, Jack Moorcroft also wore a wedding ring. He was married and that fact had made him off-limits from the day she had met him.

But even if he had not been married Margaret knew deep down she could never have fallen for him the way she had fallen for Rafe. What she couldn't quite explain was why Moorcroft could never have been the man of her dreams.

"All right, Jack, let's get the cards on the table." Margaret sat down across from her former boss at a small espresso bar table. "We both know you're not in Seattle to rehash old times."

Jack toyed with the plastic stir stick that had come with his latte. He eyed Margaret thoughtfully for a long moment. "You've changed," he said finally.

She cocked a brow, amused. "Everyone does."

"I suppose. You like the writing business?"

"Love it. But that's not what you're here to talk about, is it?"

"No." Moorcroft took a sip of the latte and set the cup down on the small table. "My information says Cassidy came to see you this week."

Margaret shrugged. "Your information is good. He was here Thursday night. What does that matter to you?"

"He wants revenge, Margaret. You know him as well, if not better than I do. You know he always gets even."

"He's already had his revenge against me. You were there that morning. You heard him tell me to get out of his life."

"But now he's back, isn't he?" Jack's mouth twisted. "Because he never got his revenge against me. He kicked you out of his bed but there wasn't much he could do to me."

Margaret felt her cheeks burn at the blunt reference to her relationship with Rafe. "Why should he want revenge against you? I was the one he thought betrayed him."

Moorcroft's eyes narrowed. "Ah, but you betrayed him to me, remember?"

"Damn it, I didn't betray anyone. I was caught in the middle and I did what I had to do."

"The way he saw it, when the chips were down, I was the one who owned your loyalty. He was right in a way, wasn't he? But he didn't like that one bit, Margaret. I think he saw me as the other man in your life."

"You were my employer, nothing more. Rafe knew that. Tell me something, Jack, did you really lie to him about us?"

Moorcroft shrugged apologetically. "Cassidy was out of control that morning. He thought what he wanted to think, which was that you felt loyal to me not only because you worked for me but because we'd been involved in an affair."

Margaret shook her head in sheer disgust. "You did lie to him."

"Does it matter if I let him think what he was already thinking? The damage had been done. He'd already thrown you out and he knew he'd lost Spencer to me."

"So you decided to take advantage of the situation and gloat over your victory."

Moorcroft smiled cryptically. "I'll admit I couldn't resist the chance to sink the knife in a little deeper. Two years ago Cassidy cost me a bundle when he wrecked a merger I had set up. I owed him."

"And I just happened to get caught in the middle this time."

"You probably don't believe this, but I'm sorry about what happened, Margaret."

"Sure. Look, let's just forget this, all right? I've got better things to do than talk over old times."

"Unfortunately I can't forget it." Moorcroft leaned forward intently. "I can't forget it because Cassidy hasn't forgotten it. He's after me."

"What are you talking about?"

"This isn't just a business rivalry between that damned cowboy and me any longer. Because of you it's turned into some kind of personal vendetta for him. A hundred years ago he would have challenged me to a showdown at high noon or some such nonsense. But we live in a civilized age now, don't we? Cassidy's going to be a bit more subtle about his vengeance."

Margaret stared at him. "What in the world are you talking about, Jack?"

Moorcroft sat hunched over his latte, his hazel eyes intent. "He's up to something, Margaret. My sources tell me he's got a deal going, a deal that could directly affect Moorcroft Industries. I need to find out what's going on before it's too late. I need inside information."

"Sound like you've already got information."

"Some. I don't know how much I can trust it."

"That's your problem, Jack."

"Look, Cassidy always plays his cards close to his chest but after what happened with you last year, he's more cautious than ever. Whatever he's working on is being kept under very tight security. I have to find out what he's up to, Margaret, before it's too late."

"Why are you coming to me about this? I don't work for you any longer, remember? I don't work for anyone except myself now. And I like it that way, Jack. I like it very much."

Moorcroft smiled. "Yes, I can see that. You look good, Margaret. Very good. I know you're out of the scene and you want to keep it that way, but I'm desperate and I need help. That business between me and Cassidy last year?"

"What about it?"

"That's all it was until you got involved. Business as usual. Cassidy and I have tangled before. Bound to happen. We're natural competitors. But after you came into the picture all that changed. Cassidy's out for blood now. Lately I've had the feeling I'm being hunted and I don't like it. I'm asking you to help me."

"You're out of your mind. I can't help you. I wouldn't even if I were in a position to do so. As you said, I'm out of this."

Moorcroft shook his head. "It's not your fault, Margaret, but the truth is, unwittingly or not, you started it. And now Cassidy is involving you again."

Margaret sat very still in her chair. "What makes you say that?"

"He's invited you down to that spread of his in Arizona, hasn't he?"

"How do you know that?"

Moorcroft sighed. "I told you, I don't have totally reliable inside information, but I have some. I've also heard your father has been seeing Beverly Cassidy."

Margaret grimaced. "Your information is better than mine, Jack. I didn't know that myself until Thursday night. My own father. I didn't even believe it at first. How could Dad . . ." She bit her lip. "Never mind."

She had spent most of Thursday night trying to convince herself that Rafe had lied to her. But several phone calls on Friday had failed to elicit any response from her father's home in California. His housekeeper had told her he had gone to Arizona.

When Margaret had angrily dialed the Cassidy ranch she had been told by another housekeeper that her father was unable to come to the phone but was looking forward to seeing her on Monday.

The unfortunate reality was that Rafe Cassidy rarely bluffed—so rarely, in fact, that when he did, he usually got away with it. Connor Lark probably was involved with Mrs. Cassidy and if that much was true, the part about selling Lark Engineering to Rafe was probably also true.

That knowledge gave Margaret a sick feeling. What was Rafe up to? she wondered.

"We're on the same side this time, Margaret." Jack's tone was soft and cajoling. "We're natural allies. Last time you were caught in the crunch. You were in love with Cassidy but you felt loyal to me. A real mess. But that's not true this time, is it? You don't owe Cassidy anything. It's payback time."

"What are you talking about? I don't want revenge, I just want out of the whole thing."

"You can't get out of it. Your father is involved. If he marries Beverly Cassidy, you're going to spend the rest of your life connected by family ties to Rafe Cassidy."

"That notion is certainly enough to kill what's left of my appetite," Margaret said morosely. The thought of being related by marriage to Rafe was mind-boggling.

Moorcroft picked up his latte and took a swallow. "You'll be going to Arizona, won't you?"

She groaned. "Probably." She had been facing that reality since Rafe had walked out the door on Thursday night. She had to find out what, exactly, was going on.

"All I'm asking is that you keep your eyes and ears open while you're down there. You may pick up something interesting, something we can both use. Maybe something that could save my hide. I'd make it worth your while, Margaret."

She looked up sharply. "Forget it, Jack. If I go down there, it won't be as your spy. I have my own reasons."

He exhaled slowly. "I understand. It was worth a shot. I'm a desperate man, Margaret. There's an outlaw on my trail and I'll do anything to survive."

"You're that afraid of Rafe?" she asked in genuine surprise.

"Like I said—before we were just business rivals. Win some, lose some. No problem. That's the name of the game. But this time things are different. This time I have a feeling I may be fighting for my life."

"Good luck."

Moorcroft turned his cup of latte carefully in his hands. He studied Margaret's face for a long moment. "You're not going to help me, are you?"

"No."

"Because you love him?"

"How I feel about Rafe has nothing to do with it. I just don't want any part of this mess, whatever it is."

"I guess I can understand that."

"Terrific," she murmured. "I'm so glad."

"Margaret, there's something I want to ask you."

She waited uneasily. "Yes?"

"If Cassidy hadn't ridden up when he did and swept you off your feet, do you think you could ever have been interested in what I had to offer?"

"You didn't have anything to offer, Jack. You're a married man, remember?"

"But if I hadn't been married?"

"My best guess is no."

"Mind telling me why not?"

"First, when I was in the business world I had a policy of never getting involved with my employers, even if they did happen to be single. From what I saw, it's almost always a bad career move for a woman to sleep with her boss. Sooner or later, she finds herself looking for another job."

"And second?"

"Let's just say you're not exactly the man of my dreams," she said dryly.

RAFE WAS WAITING at the airport gate. Margaret didn't see him at first. She was struggling with her carry-on luggage and scanning the crowd for her father. She was annoyed when she couldn't spot him. The least Connor Lark could do after causing all this commotion in her life was meet her at the airport, she told herself. When someone moved up behind her and took the travel bag from her arm, she spun around in shock.

"I'll take that for you, Maggie, love. Car's out front."

She glared up at Rafe, who was smiling down at her, a look of pure satisfaction in his gaze. He was dressed in jeans and boots and a white shirt that had the sleeves rolled up on his forearms. His hat was pulled down low over his eyes. The boots were truly spectacular—maroon leather with a beautiful turquoise and black design worked into them.

"I thought my father would have had the courtesy to meet me," she muttered.

"Don't blame Connor. I told him I'd take care of it." Rafe wrapped his hand around the nape of her neck, bent his head briefly and kissed her soundly. He did it hard and fast and allowed her no time in which to resist.

Margaret had barely registered his intentions before the whole thing was over. Scowling more furiously than ever, she stepped back quickly. She longed to slap the expression of triumph off his hard face. But at the last instant she reminded herself it would be dangerous to show any sign of a loss of self-control.

"I would appreciate it if you would not do that again," she bit out in a tight voice.

"Have a good flight?" Rafe smiled his thin, faint smile as he started down the corridor.

Margaret recalled belatedly that Rafe was very good at ignoring things he didn't care to deal with at the moment. He was already several feet away, moving in a long, rangy, ground-eating stride. She swore silently as she hurried to catch up with him. Following him was not an easy task dressed as she was in high heels and a turquoise silk suit that had an extremely narrow skirt.

"Good Lord, it's like an oven out here." Margaret gasped as she stepped through the doors of the Tucson airport terminal and into the full, humid warmth of a July day. She pulled a pair of sunglasses from her purse and glanced around at her surroundings.

The unrelenting blue of a vast desert sky arched overhead. There wasn't a cloud in sight to offer any relief from the blazing sun. Heat welled up off the pavement and poured down from above. Around her the desert stretched out in all directions, meeting the purple mountains in the distance.

"It's summer in the desert," Rafe pointed out. "What did you expect? You'll get used to it."

"Never in a million years."

"I know it's not Seattle." Rafe led the way to a silver-gray Mercedes parked in the short-term parking lot.

"Gets a little warm down here in the summer. But as I said, you get used to it."

"You might be able to get accustomed to it, but I certainly never would." It was a challenge and she knew it.

"Try, Maggie," he advised laconically. "Try real hard. You're going to be here awhile. Might as well learn to enjoy it."

"Threats already, Rafe?"

"No, ma'am. Just a little good advice." He unlocked the passenger door of the Mercedes and held it open for her.

She glared up at him as she slid into the seat. The glare turned to a wince of pain as the sun-heated leather burned through her thin silk suit.

"I'll have the air conditioner going in a minute," Rafe promised. He tossed her bags into the trunk and then got in beside her to start the Mercedes. When the car purred to life he paused for a moment with his big, capable hands on the wheel and looked at Margaret. There was a dark hunger in his eyes but it was overlaid with a cold self-control.

Margaret was grateful for the protection of her sunglasses. "How far is it to your ranch?"

"It's a few miles out of town," he said carelessly, his attention clearly on other things. "You know something? It's hard to believe you're really here. It's about time, lady."

She didn't like the way he said that. "You didn't give me much choice, did you?"

"No."

"I should have known I wasn't going to get an apology out of you."

"For what?"

"For your high-handed, arrogant, overbearing tactics," she snapped, goaded.

"Oh, those. No, you shouldn't expect an apology. I did what I had to do." He put the Mercedes in gear and pulled smoothly out of the lot. "I had to get you down here, Maggie. There wasn't any other way to do it."

"You're wasting your time, Rafe. And please stop calling me Maggie. You gave me your word you'd remember to call me Margaret."

"I said I'd try to remember."

"Try, Rafe," she murmured, mimicking his earlier words. "Try real hard."

Rafe gave her an amused look as he stopped to hand some cash to the gate attendant. "But I've got a lot on my mind these days and the small stuff tends to slip through the cracks."

Her hands clenched in her lap. "That's all I ever was to you, wasn't it, Rafe? Small stuff. Unimportant stuff."

"You're small, all right." His voice had an affectionate, teasing edge to it now as he pulled away from the gate. "But no way are you going to slip through the cracks. Not this time."

"You don't want me back, Rafe."

"No? Why would I go to all the bother of blackmail to get you here if I didn't want you back?"

She frowned. "I've been thinking about that. The only conclusion I can come up with is that in your mind I'm the one who got away. It's true you kicked me out of your life, but when I went without a backward glance and stayed out, your ego took a beating, didn't it?"

"You did a number on my ego, all right," he agreed dryly. "It hasn't been the same since."

"Is that what this is all about? Revenge?" She shivered, remembering what Jack Moorcroft had said. *Cassidy is out for blood.*

"I would do a lot of things for revenge under certain circumstances," Rafe said, "but getting married isn't one of them. I'm not masochistic. Don't make any mistake about it, Maggie. I brought you down here to give myself some time to undue the damage that got done last year."

"The damage is irreparable."

"No, it's not. We're going to put that mess behind us and get on with our lives."

"I have been getting on with my life," she pointed out. "Very nicely, thank you. I've been quite happy this past year."

"Lucky you. I've been to hell and back."

She sucked in her breath. "Rafe, please, don't say things like that. We both know you're not the type to pine for a woman, especially one you think betrayed you. You're far more likely to look for a way to reap some vengeance against her. And I suspect that's exactly what you're doing by going after my father's firm."

"I'm not going after it. Your dad wants to sell to me. It's a profitable operation that will fit in well with the other businesses Cassidy and Company runs, so I'm taking a serious look at it. That's all there is to it."

"I don't believe that."

"I know. That's why you're here, isn't it? To rescue Connor from my clutches. You might be able to do that, Maggie, but I doubt you'll get him out of my mother's hands. Wait until you see them together. They're made for each other."

"It's all part of some plot you've cooked up, Rafe. Why don't you tell me what you're really after?"

"You're beginning to sound paranoid, honey."

"I'm not paranoid, I'm careful."

He smiled fleetingly at that. "No, Maggie, you're not careful. If you were careful, you wouldn't be here."

Margaret took refuge in silence for the next several miles. She folded her arms beneath her breasts and stared out the window at the arid landscape as she tried desperately to think. She had been struggling to put together some sort of battle plan ever since she had accepted the inevitability of this trip. But she was still very uncertain of what to do now that she was here. Part of the problem was that she could not be sure of what Rafe was really up to.

She did not believe for a moment that he wanted to marry her. But it was entirely possible he wanted to seduce her so that he could have the satisfaction of punishing her for her so-called betrayal.

Then, too, there was Moorcroft to consider. She didn't care what happened to Jack or his firm but she had to wonder if Rafe intended to use her in some scheme to get even with his rival.

Finally there was the business of her father getting involved with Beverly Cassidy and planning to sell Lark Engineering to Rafe.

No doubt about it, the situation was complicated and potentially dangerous.

A typical Rafe Cassidy operation, Margaret thought.

3

"THIS IS YOUR HOME, Rafe?" Margaret watched in amazement as the main buildings of the Cassidy Ranch came into view.

Set in the foothills with a sweeping view of Tucson in the distance, the ranch was an impressive sight. At the end of a long, winding drive was a graceful house done in the classic Spanish Colonial style. The walls had the look of warm, earth-toned adobe and the roof was red tile. Lush greenery surrounded the place, a welcome antidote to the rugged desert landscape. Low, white, modern-looking barns, white fences and green pastures spread out from the house. Margaret could see horses in the fields.

"Things were a little rushed during that two-month period after we met," Rafe reminded her coolly. "There wasn't time to get you down here to see the place before you . . . left me."

"You mean before you threw me out of your life."

Rafe drew a breath. "It was an argument, Maggie. A bad one. I lost my temper and said a lot of things I didn't mean."

"Oh, you meant them, all right. Where are the cows?" Margaret added in mild curiosity. "Shouldn't there be cows on a ranch like this?"

"This time of year the cattle are scattered all to hell and gone up in the foothills," Rafe said impatiently.

"Why so many horses? They don't look like quarter horses."

"They aren't. They're Arabians. We breed them. Some of the best in the world. The profit margin is a lot more reliable than cattle. In fact, I'm thinking of getting out of the cattle business altogether."

"Well, that figures. I don't see you getting involved in anything that doesn't show an excellent profit margin. Have you considered chickens?"

"*Chickens?*" His expression was a mask of outrage, the sort of outrage only a true cattleman could manage.

"Sure. Red meat is out, Rafe. Haven't you been following the latest health advice? Chicken, fish and vegetables are in. Oh, and turkeys. You might try raising turkeys. I understand they're not real bright so you should be able to figure out a way to round them up and brand them if you feel you must maintain the old traditions."

"Forget chickens and forget turkeys," he growled.

"All right. I imagine the real basis for the family fortune is Cassidy and Company anyway, isn't it? You rustle companies now instead of cattle."

Rafe slanted her a brief, annoyed glance as he parked the Mercedes. "You're determined to make this difficult, aren't you?"

"As difficult as I can," she assured him as she opened her own car door and got out. "Where is my father?"

"Probably out by the pool. That's where I left him when I went to get you." Rafe got out of the Mercedes just as a young man wearing a striped shirt and black jeans came around the corner of the house. "Tom, this is Maggie Lark. Maggie, this is Tom. He takes care of the house gardens and a lot of other odds and ends around here. Tom, grab the lady's luggage, will you? It goes into the south guest bedroom."

"Sure thing, Rafe. Afternoon, Miss Lark. We've been expecting you. Have a good trip?"

"Fine, thank you, Tom." Margaret smiled coolly at him. "Where is the pool?"

Tom looked surprised. "The pool? Out in the patio. Straight through the house. But don't you want to settle into your room first? Maybe change your clothes?" He eyed her silk suit dubiously.

"I want to see my father first. This is a business trip as far as I'm concerned."

"Oh, yeah. Sure. Business." Tom was obviously baffled by that statement. "Like I said, right through the middle of the house."

Margaret did not wait for Rafe to do the honors. She felt his sardonic gaze on her as she turned and strode straight toward the wide, dark wooden door of the Spanish-style home. She opened it and found herself in a cool, tiled hall. The air-conditioning felt wonderful. She took off her sunglasses and glanced around with unwilling curiosity.

This was Rafe's hideaway, she knew, the Cassidy family ranch. He had mentioned it once or twice during the brief time she had been dating him. It was the place he came to when the pressure of his fast-track lifestyle occasionally caught up with him. That wasn't often. Rafe's stamina was legendary.

The Southwestern style of the outside of Rafe's home had been carried on inside. Soft earthtones, terra cotta, peach and pale turquoise dominated. Here and there was a shot of black in the form of a vase or a lamp. Heavily beamed ceilings and rugs with geometric Indian designs woven into them gave a rustic effect that was also surprisingly gracious.

Through the floor-to-ceiling windows that lined one entire wall of the long living room Margaret could see the pool. It occupied the center of a beautifully landscaped courtyard that was enclosed by the four wings of the house. Two figures were seated under an umbrella, a pitcher of tea on the table between them. Connor Lark and Beverly Cassidy were laughing in delight over some private joke.

Margaret watched the couple for a moment, uncertainty seizing her insides. Her father looked happy— happier than she had ever seen him since her mother died several years ago. She sensed suddenly that her mission to rescue him was going to be difficult to carry out.

"What's the matter, Maggie? Afraid it's not going to be so simple after all?" Rafe asked as he walked into the hall behind her. "I told you they were made for each other."

She glanced back at him, her eyes narrowing. "Hard to imagine you as a matchmaker, Rafe."

"You think I arranged for them to fall for each other just to make it easier to get my hands on Lark Engineering?" He sounded amused. "I'm good, Maggie, but I'm not that good. I take full responsibility for introducing them. After that, they did it all by themselves."

"You think you're very clever, don't you?"

"If I were really clever, we wouldn't have wasted a year of our lives apart. Look, Maggie, do everyone a favor and don't take your father's relationship with my mother as a personal threat, okay? The fact that he fell in love with her doesn't translate directly into a betrayal of you. It's not like your father has gone over to the enemy camp."

Her fingers tightened on the strap of her purse as the shot went home. A part of her had been viewing the situation in exactly that light, she acknowledged privately. It was irrational but the feeling was there on some level. "My father was already halfway into the enemy camp before he met your mother. He took to you right from the start, didn't he?"

"He thought I'd make you a good husband. He was right."

"Oh, yes, he thought you were the ideal husband for me. A genuine cowboy. The son he'd never had, or something along those lines I imagine. I swear, if he'd had the power to arrange the marriage, I think he would have done it. Lark Engineering would have been my dowry."

"There is something to be said for arranged marriages, isn't there?"

"This is not a joke, Rafe."

"So Connor and I get along." Rafe leaned against the wall and folded his arms. "So what?"

Margaret smiled grimly. "Well, at least I've got one person on my side."

"Who?" His eyes were taunting.

"Your mother. She must have been enormously relieved when you threw me out of your life last year."

The lines of his face hardened. "Don't count on it. And stop saying I threw you out."

"That's what happened."

"It was your damn pride that screwed everything up, and you know it. If you'd had the grace to admit you were wrong a year ago, we could have worked things out."

"I wasn't wrong. I did what I had to do. If you'd had the decency not to use me in your campaign to beat Moorcroft to Spencer in the first place, the entire situation would never have developed."

Rafe swore softly and then straightened away from the wall as Tom approached with the luggage. "Go say hello to your father, Maggie."

Feeling a little more cheerful because it seemed like she'd just won that round, Maggie crossed the living room and opened one of the glass doors. Her father looked up as she stepped onto the patio.

"Maggie, my girl, you're here. It's about time. Come on over and have some tea. Bev and I've been waitin' for you to come rescue me from Cassidy's clutches. Good to see you, girl, good to see you. Been a while since we talked."

"We could have had a nice long talk if you'd bothered to answer the phone when I called down here to see what was going on."

"Now, Maggie, girl, don't go gettin' on your high horse. I only did what I thought was best. You know that."

It was impossible to hold on to her anger when her father looked at her with such delight. Margaret saw the relaxed good humor in his eyes and she sighed inwardly. No question about it, her father was here of his own free will.

Connor Lark was a big man, almost as big as Rafe, and he was built like a mountain. There was a hint of a belly cantilevered out over the waistband of his swimming trunks, but he still looked very solid. His black hair had long since turned silver and his aqua eyes, so like her own, were as lively as ever.

Margaret's mother had always claimed he was a diamond in the rough whom she'd had to spend a great deal of time polishing. Connor always claimed she'd enjoyed every minute of the task and Margaret knew she had. From a desperately poor background as a rancher, Connor had risen to become a self-made entrepreneur who had built Lark Engineering into a thriving modern business.

"Well, Dad. Looks like you're enjoying the process of selling out." Margaret smiled affectionately at her father and then turned a slightly wary smile on the attractive woman who sat on the other side of the table. "Hello, Bev. Nice to see you again."

Rafe's mother was a trim, energetic-looking woman who was approximately the same age as Connor, although she looked younger. Her short, well-styled hair was the color of fine champagne. She was wearing a black-and-white swimsuit cover-up and a pair of leather sandals that projected an image of subtle elegance, even though they constituted sportswear. Bev's expression was gracious but her pale gray eyes held the same hint of wariness Margaret knew were in her own.

"Hello, Margaret. I'm pleased to see you again."

Margaret leaned down to kiss her father's cheek, thinking that she and Bev were both good at social lies. She was well aware she had not made a particularly good impression on Beverly Cassidy on the one occasion they had met last year. There was an excellent reason for that. Bev Cassidy had not considered Margaret a good candidate as a wife for her one and only son. Margaret tended to agree with her.

"Do sit down, Margaret," Bev said, reaching for the pitcher of iced tea and pouring her guest a glass. "You must be exhausted from your trip. Your father and I just finished a swim. After you've said hello you must go and put on your suit. I'm sure a dip in the pool will feel good." She turned her welcoming smile on her son as Rafe came through the glass doors and followed Margaret to the shaded loungers. "Oh, there you are, Rafe. Iced tea?"

"Thanks."

He held out his hand for the glass as he sat down beside Margaret on one of the loungers. His powerfully muscled thigh brushed her leg and Margaret promptly shifted to put a few more inches between them. He ignored the small retreat.

Margaret took a long, fortifying sip of iced tea and studied the three people who surrounded her. Her father and Bev appeared to be waiting for her to make the next move. Rafe didn't look particularly concerned one way or the other. To look at him one would have thought this was a perfectly normal family gathering. Margaret frowned over her glass.

"Why don't we all stop playing games," she suggested in a voice that she hoped hid her own inner tension. "We all know this isn't a happy little poolside party."

"Speak for yourself," Connor suggested easily. "I'm happy." He reached across the table and caught Bev's hand, smiling at the older woman. "And I think Bev is, too. Did Rafe tell you the good news?"

"That you and Bev are involved? Yes, he did."

Connor scowled slightly. "I don't know about *involved*. I'm not up on all the new terminology. Is that what they call plannin' to get married nowadays?"

Margaret swallowed. Rafe had been right. This was serious. "You're planning marriage?"

"Yes, we are." Bev looked at Margaret with a faint air of challenge. "I hope you approve."

"I wish you both the best," Margaret made herself say politely. "You'll understand that the news has come as something of a shock. I had no idea you two had even met until Rafe mentioned it."

"Take it easy, Maggie, girl," Connor said gently. "There were reasons I didn't want to talk about it until now."

"Reasons?" She pinned him with her gaze.

"Now, Maggie, lass, you know what I'm talkin' about. The situation 'tween you and Rafe here has been a mite tense for some time."

Margaret arched her brows and slid a long, assessing glance at Rafe. "Tense? I wouldn't say that. I wasn't particularly tense at all during the past year. Were you tense, Rafe?"

"I had my moments," he muttered.

She nodded. "Well, I did try to warn you about stress, didn't I? As I recall, I gave you several pithy little lectures about your long hours, non-existent vacations and general tendency to put your work first."

"I believe you did mention the subject. Several times, in fact."

Margaret smiled coldly. "Come now, Rafe, you can be honest in front of Dad and your mother. Admit the full truth. Toward the end there I was starting to turn into a full-blown nag when it came to the matter of your total devotion to work, wasn't I? I think I was even beginning to threaten you that if our relationship didn't get equal time there wouldn't be a relationship."

Bev shifted uneasily in her chair, her eyes swinging to Connor.

Margaret's father whistled soundlessly. "Oh, ho. So that's the way of it, is it?"

Rafe gave Margaret a repressive stare. "I had my hands full last year when we met, if you'll recall. I was juggling a couple of companies that were valued in the millions. Things are different now. I'm making some changes in my life."

"Such as?"

"I've cut way back on the juggling, for one thing." He flashed her a quick grin.

Margaret was not amused. "I find that hard to believe."

"Hey, I'm down here in Arizona with you, aren't I?" He smiled again. "Two full weeks, maybe three if I get lucky. You have my full attention, Maggie, love."

"Not quite. You're in the middle of negotiating a deal with my father, remember?"

Connor chuckled. "She's got you there, Rafe. We are supposed to be talking business off and on, aren't we?"

"Speaking of this little matter of selling the company you built with the sweat of your brow, Dad, just what is going on?" Margaret pinned her father with a quelling glare.

"What can I tell you?" Connor shrugged massively. "It's the truth. If I can get a decent offer out of Cassidy, here, Lark Engineering is his."

"But, Dad, you never told me you were thinking of selling."

"The time has come to enjoy some of the money I made with all that brow sweat. Bev and I plan to do a lot of traveling and a fair amount of just plain fooling around. I'm even looking at a nifty little yacht. Can't you just see me in that fancy yachting getup?"

"But the company has always been so important to you, Dad."

"It's still important. Maggie, girl, I'll be perfectly truthful with you. If you'd stayed in the business world, shown a real interest in it, I'd probably have turned it over to you one of these days. But let's face it, girl, you aren't cut out for that world. And now you've got yourself a fine new career, one you've taken to like a duck to water. I'm glad for you, but it leaves me with a problem. I've got to do something with the firm."

"So you're just going to hand it over to Rafe?"

"He's not exactly handing it over," Rafe muttered. "Your father is holding me at gunpoint. You ought to hear what he's asking for Lark."

"I see." Margaret felt some of the righteous determination seep out of her. Everything was already beyond her control. Rafe was in command, as usual. Things would go his way. A curious sense of inevitability began to come over her. Determinedly she fought back. "Where's the ubiquitous Hatcher?" Margaret asked, glancing meaningfully around the pool. "Surely you haven't dismissed your faithful, loyal, ever-present assistant for two solid weeks?"

Rafe took a swallow of tea. "Hatcher is going to drop by occasionally to brief me on how things are going at the main office. But that's all. I've delegated almost everything else. I'm only available for world-class emergencies. Satisfied?"

"You don't have to worry about my feelings on the subject," Margaret said. "Not anymore. You're free to run your life any way you choose."

"Ouch." Connor winced.

"I know what you mean," Rafe remarked. "She's been sniping at me like that every chance she gets. But I've promised myself I'll be tolerant, patient and understanding. She can't keep it up forever."

"Don't bet on it." Margaret got to her feet. "I believe I will have that swim now. If you'll excuse me, Bev?"

"Of course, dear. The water is lovely."

Bev looked relieved to see her go. But there was an unexpected trace of unhappiness in her gaze, too, Margaret noticed. She wondered about that as she turned to walk back into the house. Surely after the things Bev Cassidy had said to her last year, she couldn't be hoping for a reconciliation between her son and his errant mistress.

Mistress. The old-fashioned word still burned in Margaret's ears whenever she remembered Bev's last words to her. *You'd make him a better mistress than you would a wife.*

"Cocktails at six out here by the pool, dear," Bev called after her. "We'll be eating around seven-thirty. Connor and Rafe have promised to grill us some steaks."

"Right," Connor said cheerfully. "Got us some of the biggest, juiciest, thickest steaks on the face of the planet."

Margaret laughed for the first time since Thursday night. She looked back at the small group gathered under the umbrella. "I almost forgot to mention that I've made a few life-style changes myself during the past year."

"Such as?" Rafe asked, lion's eyes watchful.

"I never touch red meat." Margaret walked on into the cool house, paying no attention to her father's bellow of astonishment.

SHORTLY AFTER ONE O'CLOCK in the morning, Margaret eased open the patio door of her bedroom and slipped out into the silent courtyard. She had changed into her bathing suit a few minutes earlier, finally admitting that she was not going to be able to sleep.

The balmy desert air was still amazingly warm. It carried a myriad of soft scents from the gardens. Overhead, the star-studded sky stretched into a dark infinity. Margaret had the feeling that if she listened closely she might actually be able to hear a coyote howl from some nearby hilltop.

The underwater lights of the swimming pool glowed invitingly. Margaret slipped off her sandals and slid into the water. She hovered weightlessly for a long moment and then began to swim the length of the pool. The tension in her muscles slowly dissolved.

It had been a difficult evening.

If she had any sense she would leave tomorrow, she told herself as she reached the far end of the pool and started back. It was the only thing to do. Her father was happy. It was obvious he was not being bamboozled out of Lark Engineering. He truly wanted to sell out to Rafe so there was nothing she could say or do. It was his business, after all.

Yes, she should definitely leave tomorrow. But every time she felt Rafe's eyes on her she found herself looking for an excuse to stay. The excuse of doing battle with him was the only one she had.

There was no sound behind her on the flagstone but something made Margaret pause in the water and look back toward the far side of the pool. Rafe stood there in the shadows clad in only a snug-fitting pair of swim trunks. Moonlight gleamed on his broad shoulders and in the darkness his eyes were watchful and mysterious.

"Couldn't sleep?" he asked softly.

"No." She treaded water wondering if she should flee back to the safety of her bedroom. But she seemed to lack the strength of will to get out of the pool.

"Neither could I. I've been lying in bed wondering what kind of reception I'd get if I went to your bedroom."

"A very cold reception."

"You think so? I'm not so sure. That's what was keeping me awake, you know. The uncertainty." He lowered himself silently into the water and stroked quietly toward her.

Margaret instinctively edged back until her shoulders were against the side of the pool. She gripped the tiled edge with one hand as Rafe came to a halt in front of her. "Rafe, I don't think this is a good idea. I came out here to swim alone."

"You're not alone any longer." He put his hands on either side of her, gripping the tile and effectively caging her against the side of the pool. But he made no move to bring his body against hers.

"Are you trying to intimidate me?" Margaret asked, shockingly aware of the brush of his leg against hers under water. Old memories, never far from the surface, welled up swiftly, bringing with them the jolt of desire.

"My goal isn't to intimidate you, honey, it's to remind you of a few things," Rafe said gently. "A few very good things." He came closer, causing the water to lap softly at her throat and shoulders. "Maggie, I've wanted you back in my bed every night since you left. Every damned night. Doesn't that mean anything to you?"

She shivered, although the water was warm. "Did you mean what you said last Thursday? There hasn't been anyone else since you and I . . . since we've been apart?"

"I meant it. The only thing that kept me sane was knowing you weren't sleeping with anyone else, either."

She scowled. "How did you know that, anyway?"

His mouth thinned. "It's not important."

"You aren't just guessing about my lovelife during the past year, are you? You know for a fact I haven't been serious about anyone else. Damn it, Rafe, there's only one way you could be so certain. You hired someone to spy on me, didn't you?"

"Maggie, honey, I told you, it's not important."

"Well, it's very important to me. Rafe, how could you?"

"Hush, love." His hand wrapped around her nape and he kissed her lightly. "I said it's not important. Not any longer."

"You should be ashamed of yourself."

"Have pity on me, love. I was a desperate man."

"Rafe, the last thing I will ever have for you is pity. Just what did you think you were going to do if I got involved with someone else?" she demanded.

"Could we discuss something else? Your voice is rising. If you're not careful, you'll wake Mom and Connor. Their bedrooms open onto this courtyard, too."

The last thing she wanted was for anyone to overhear this particular conversation. Margaret reluctantly lowered her tone to a fierce whisper. "What did you think you were going to do, Rafe?"

"Move our thrilling reconciliation up a few months," he told her wryly.

"You're impossible." She didn't believe for a moment that was all he would have done. It was becoming very clear that Rafe had never stopped thinking of her as belonging to him during the past year. Only the knowledge that he'd been celibate during that entire time himself kept her from going up in flames over the matter.

"Tell me you missed me, Maggie. Just a little?"

She shook her head mutely.

"Admit it," Rafe urged, moving a little closer in the water. "Give me that much, honey."

"No." The single word was a soft gasp of dismay. He was only inches from her now. His hands were on either side of her, trapping her.

"You remember how good it was, don't you, love?" He kissed her fleetingly again, closing the distance between them until there wasn't any at all. "I didn't go looking for anyone else because I knew it would be useless. You knew there wasn't anyone else for you, either, didn't you?"

"Oh, Rafe." She muttered his name in a soft cry that was part protest, part acceptance of a truth that could not be denied.

"Yeah, Maggie, love. You do remember, don't you? A whole year, sweetheart. A year of pure hell."

Margaret felt his leg slide between hers as his mouth came down to claim her lips. She felt her breasts being softly crushed against his chest. The hot, sweet rain of passion too long denied swept through her, pooling just below her stomach. Rafe was the only man who had ever been able to do this to her, the only one who could bring her to such shockingly intense arousal with only a look and a kiss and a touch.

Nothing had changed.

"Maggie, love, this time we'll make things work between us." Rafe's mouth moved on hers, gliding along the line of her jaw up to the lobe of her ear. He bit gently, tantalizing her with a pleasure that was not quite pain. "Just give me a chance, sweetheart. I'm going to prove it. Everything is going to be different this time around. Except for this part. No need to fix this, is there?"

He was right about one thing, Margaret thought. This part was still very, very good. Slowly, with a growing sense of inevitability, she felt herself sliding back into the magic world of sensuality that she had shared all too briefly with Rafe.

"Let me love you, Maggie. Let me hold you the way I used to hold you."

"Back when I was your mistress?"

He shook his head, his gaze suddenly fierce. "I never thought of you as a mistress. You were the woman I was going to marry. I knew that from the first day I met you."

"Your mother said I would make a better mistress for you than I would a wife and I think she may have been right."

Rafe's head came up abruptly. "What the devil are you talking about?"

"Never mind. As you said a minute ago, it's not important."

"Maggie, stop talking in riddles."

"I've got a better idea," she suggested softly. "Let's not talk at all." She put her arms around his neck as she made her decision. Heaven help her, she did not have the power to deny herself a night in Rafe's arms. "You were right, Rafe. This part was always very good." She brushed her lips lightly across his and felt his shudder of response.

"Maggie, love." Rafe's voice was a husky groan. "Are you telling me the waiting is over?"

"I want you, Rafe. I never stopped wanting you."

Rafe's mouth closed over hers once more, hard and passionate and filled with a year's worth of pent-up need. Margaret felt his hands moving on her under the water, relearning the shape and feel of her.

His tongue surged between her lips as his fingers slipped under the edge of her swimming suit bra. She gasped as she felt his thumbs slide over her nipples.

"Rafe?"

"Not here," he muttered. "Too much chance of an audience. I'm taking you back to my room."

He hauled himself up onto the tiled edge of the pool with easy strength, then reached down and lifted her up beside him. Margaret looked up into his dark eyes and saw the undiluted hunger there. She felt the answering ache of desire within herself and knew she was still in love with Rafe Cassidy.

You'd make him a better mistress than a wife.

Bev Cassidy's words rang in Margaret's ears once more as Rafe swept her up into his arms and started toward the open door of his bedroom.

4

THE BEDROOM WAS FILLED with the inviting mysteries of the night. The woman in Rafe's arms was intoxicating and seemed a part of that glittering darkness.

He was only half conscious of the dark, cool shadows and the pooling white sheets on the wide bed. All Rafe could think of now was the warm, sensual weight of the woman he held. *His woman.* She was finally back where she belonged.

"It's been so long," he muttered thickly as he set her down beside the bed and reached for a towel. "Too damn long."

He used the towel carefully, tenderly, lovingly. He squeezed the moisture out of her hair and then combed the damp strands back from her forehead with his fingers. She had a misty look on her face. She smiled at him and kissed him gently.

He stroked the water droplets off her arms and knelt to sleek it from her long, curving legs. As he worked he touched her, aware of a surging sense of pure delight as he trailed his fingers along her smooth skin.

When he was finished he quickly dried himself and tossed the towel aside. Then he reached for her.

"Maggie, love. My sweet, sexy Maggie." He pulled her against his chest until her head was resting on his shoulder and then he undid the fastening of her swimsuit bra. Carefully he pulled it free, sliding the straps off her shoulders. He looked down and saw the hardened tips of her breasts and for an instant he thought the desire would overcome him then and there.

It took all his self-control not to rush. He stroked her the way he would one of his beautiful, sensitive mares—gently and slowly. She responded at once, vividly, the way she always had to his touch. Her reaction only served to enhance his own. When her lips moved against his bare skin and her arms went around his waist, he shuddered.

"I missed you so, Rafe."

The soft admission nearly sent him over the edge. "Oh, babe." His fingers trembled as he slid them under the edge of her bikini and pushed the scrap of material down over her hips. It fell to the floor and she stepped daintily away from the damp fabric.

Rafe took a deep breath as he looked down at her. "You're more lovely than you were even in my dreams. And believe me I had a few that were so hot I'm amazed you didn't feel the flames all the way up there in Seattle."

"I had a few of my own." Her eyes were luminous in the shadows as she slid her fingers through the hair on his chest. She traced the shape of his shoulders and then her palm shaped the muscles of his upper arms.

Rafe couldn't wait any longer. He picked her up and set her down on the bed. He felt heavy, his body taut with arousal. His mind whirled with it. He stripped off his swim trunks and lowered himself down beside her. Then he flattened his palm on her stomach and moved his fingers into the triangle of curls at the junction of her thighs. Suddenly his hand was still.

"Rafe, what's wrong?" Margaret asked softly.

"Nothing. Nothing's wrong." He bent his head and tasted one full nipple. The sensation was exquisite. "I'm just half out of my mind with wanting you now that I've finally got you back in my bed. But I want to do this right. I intended to take it slow. I've waited this long to make it perfect for you."

She laughed, a soft, throaty sound that made him want to hug her. "Rafe, it was always so good, no matter how we did it—fast, slow or in between. You don't have to worry about how we do it tonight."

He groaned and kissed her throat. "Touch me, baby. Feel how much I want you."

Her gentle fingers closed around him and Rafe sucked in his breath, his eyes slitting in reaction to the caress. "You're right. It was good any way we did it and there's no way I can take it slow tonight." He reached over and yanked open the drawer in the nightstand, groping for the small box he had optimistically put there earlier. He used one hand and his teeth to open the packet so he could keep the other hand on Maggie's thigh. He didn't want to let go of her for a second.

A moment later he moved again, rolling on top of Maggie with the wild eagerness of a stallion. He tried to control himself but she was reaching up to clasp him to her and her willingness was his undoing. He parted her legs with his own.

"Yes, Rafe. Please."

He felt her silken thighs alongside his hips and a near-violent wave of desire surged through him. When he probed her carefully he met the damp, welcoming heat and that was all he could stand. He guided himself into her, driving forward into her core. She was so tight. He wondered if he should stop and give her time to adjust to him. After all, it had been a whole year.

But he couldn't stop. Not now. He needed to bury himself within her. Rafe moaned as he slid fully into her depths. He heard her soft cry in his ear and her nails dug into his shoulders.

"Am I hurting you?" he asked, his breathing turning ragged.

"No. No, it feels wonderful. It's just...been a while, that's all."

"Too damn long for both of us."

"Yes." She lifted her hips against him, telling him she was ready now, urging him into the ancient rhythm.

Rafe needed no additional coaxing. He held her so tightly he was half afraid of crushing her. But she clung to him just as fiercely. He sank himself again and again into her heat until he felt her tightening around him in the old, familiar way.

"*Rafe.*"

"That's it, Maggie, love," he muttered against her mouth. "Come on, honey. Go wild for me."

She shivered and cried out again. He opened his mouth over hers and swallowed the soft, sweet sound. She bucked beneath him and he groaned heavily. Nothing had ever been as shatteringly sexy to Rafe as the feel of Maggie climaxing beneath him.

He waited until the last of the tremors were fading and then he slammed into her one more time and felt himself explode.

Rafe rode the storm for what seemed like forever, the passion in him apparently limitless. And then it was over. He relaxed heavily on top of Maggie, squashing her into the damp sheets.

His last coherent thought was that the waiting and planning were finally finished. He had his Maggie back. No one had ever made him feel the way Maggie did.

It was a long time before Rafe reluctantly stirred. He only did so because he felt Maggie pushing experimentally against his shoulder.

"What's wrong?" he mumbled, half asleep.

"You're getting very heavy."

"Nag, nag, nag." He levered himself slowly away from her and rolled onto his back. He cradled her close to his side and yawned. "Better?"

"Umm-hmm." She kissed his jaw and then his shoulder, her lips incredibly soft against his skin. "I'd better get back to my own room before I fall asleep."

"No," he muttered instantly. He opened one eye to glare at her. "You sleep here."

She smiled. "I think it would be better if I went back to my own room."

"Why?" He was beginning to feel belligerent.

"Because we aren't alone in the house, remember?"

"My mother and your father both know we've had an affair in the not so distant past and they both know why you're here now. They're not going to ask any questions about why you spent the night in my room. They've taken more than one weekend trip together, you know. Hell, I wouldn't be surprised if your father is paying a late night visit to my mother even as we speak."

"Even if he is, you can bet he'll be back in his own room by dawn. That's the way their generation does things. It's a matter of propriety."

"Yeah? Well, our generation is different."

She chuckled softly. "I'm not so sure about that." Her eyes sobered. "Please, Rafe. I think it would be better if I go back to my own room. It would be embarrassing for me in the morning if . . ." Her voice trailed off abruptly.

Rafe grinned knowingly and ran his fingers through her hair. "You mean if everyone in the house finds out you surrendered after only one night back under my roof? Yeah, I can see where that would be a little embarrassing for you."

She poked him in the ribs and scowled. "I did not surrender."

Her eyes searched his face. She looked as if she was about to say something and changed her mind. "Good night, Rafe."

He didn't like it but he didn't want to argue with her. Not now that things were finally all right again. "You always were a little shy about this kind of thing, weren't you?"

"I prefer to think of it as circumspect."

"Downright prudish if you ask me. You know what? You're just an old-fashioned girl at heart. But I guess I can put up with your modesty until we make things official." He dragged her head down for another slow, deep kiss and then he forced himself to his feet. He stretched broadly, flexing his muscles for the sheer physical pleasure of it. He hadn't felt this good in a long, long time. A year, to be exact.

"You don't have to walk me back to my room. It's just across the patio. Won't take me ten seconds to get there." Margaret was already reaching for her swimsuit and a towel. He watched her fasten the bra of the suit and wrap the towel around her waist.

"Hey, you're not the only old-fashioned one around here. I'm a little old-fashioned myself. I always walk my dates home, if I can't persuade them to stay until morning." He spoke lightly but when she gave him a strange, searching glance, he frowned. "Something wrong?"

She shook her head quickly, her still damp hair clinging beguilingly to her throat. "No. I was just remembering something someone had said to me a couple of days ago at a book signing session. Something about cowboys being old-fashioned when it came to things like women."

"Yeah, well, that's what I am when you come right down to it, Maggie, love. A cowboy."

"But you're a very modern sort of cowboy," she said, as if trying to convince herself of something. "You run a large corporation and you routinely make multimillion-dollar deals."

"I can also work cattle and break a horse."

"You can order good wine when the occasion calls for it."

"Yeah, but I don't drink it unless somebody's holding a gun to my head."

"You know the best hotels to stay in when you travel."

"I can also build a fire and skin a rabbit."

"Rafe, I'm trying to make a point here."

"So? What's the fact that I can move in two different worlds got to do with anything? Once a cowboy, always a cowboy. Take a look at your father. He was born and raised on a ranch. He may have gotten an engineering degree but that doesn't change what he is deep down inside. That's one of the reasons he and I get along. We understand each other."

"Oh, what's the use. You may be right. I have to tell you the truth, Rafe. I never wanted to get involved with a cowboy, modern or otherwise."

"Too bad, Maggie, love, because you are involved with one. For your own sake, don't go trying to convince yourself you've gotten hooked up with one of those new, sensitive, right-thinking males you read about in ladies' magazines."

Margaret wrinkled her nose. "What would you know about the new, sensitive, right-thinking man? You don't read women's magazines."

"I heard all about 'em from Julie once when she was trying to convince me to approve of some damned psychologist she was dating."

"Rafe, did you ruin that relationship for her?"

"I didn't have to. The guy ruined it for himself. She found out he was seeing someone else on the side and when she confronted him he told her he needed a relationship in which he could be free to explore his full potential as a human being."

Margaret eyed him curiously. "What happened?"

"What do you think happened? Julie's a Cassidy, too. Cassidys don't believe in open relationships. She gave him a swift kick in his new, sensitive, right-thinking rear."

"Good for her," Margaret said automatically and then frowned darkly. "Still, you shouldn't judge the new, sensitive, right-thinking man by one bad apple, Rafe."

"I'm not going to judge the new, sensitive, right-thinking man at all. I'm going to ignore him and so are you." He bent his head and brushed her lips with his own.

Her mouth was still full and soft from the after-effects of their recent lovemaking. The scent of her hung in the room and would be clinging to his sheets. Rafe felt himself getting hard all over again just thinking about what was going to happen to him when he climbed back into those sheets.

"Rafe?"

"You're sure you want to go?"

"Yes."

"As I said, I can wait. I'm one hell of a patient man, Maggie, love." He pulled on his trunks, took her hand and led her out into the starlit patio.

MARGARET ROSE VERY EARLY the next morning after a restless night's sleep. Her thoughts, confused and chaotic, had tumbled about in her head after Rafe had left her to return to his own room. She could not regret their lovemaking or the resumption of their precarious relationship, but she knew there was trouble on the horizon.

There were too many unresolved issues, too many things from the past that had not changed. Rafe was still Rafe. And that meant there would be problems.

Still, this morning she could allow herself to think more positively about the possibilities of an affair with the man she loved. She would never find anyone else like him, Margaret knew.

She chose a pair of designer jeans that were cut to show off her small waist and emphasize the flare of her hips. She added a rakish red shirt and sandals and went out into the patio to savor the short cool hours of early morning in the desert. Soon the temperature would start climbing rapidly.

"Good morning, Margaret. Come and join me in a cup of coffee."

Margaret glanced in surprise at Bev Cassidy who was sitting alone under the umbrella. A stout-looking woman in her fifties had just finished putting a silver pot of coffee and a tray of fresh breakfast pastries and fruit down on the table. The woman smiled at Margaret and nodded a greeting. Margaret smiled back.

"Margaret, this is Ellen. Ellen comes in during the days to take care of the house for Rafe."

"Ellen."

"Nice to meet you, Miss Lark. Hope you enjoy your stay. By the way, I love your books."

"Thank you very much."

"Sit down," Bev urged as the housekeeper disappeared.

"You're up bright and early, Bev." Margaret summoned up a smile and walked over to take a seat opposite her hostess. She had known when she had boarded the plane that there would be no way to avoid Rafe's mother. She braced herself for this first one-on-one confrontation.

"I love the early hours in the desert." Bev poured a cup of coffee and handed it to Margaret. "Did you sleep well, dear?"

Margaret took refuge in a social white lie. "Very well, thank you."

Bev smiled gently. "I'm sorry you had to learn about your father's engagement the way you did. Rafe was very insistent on keeping the full truth from you until . . ." She let the words slide away into nothingness.

"Until he was ready to close his trap?" Margaret nodded as she sipped her coffee. "That's Rafe, all right. Sneaky." She reached for a slice of melon.

Bev let out a small sigh. "He cares very deeply about you, Margaret. I hadn't fully realized just how much until you left him last year."

"I would like to clear up a major misconception around here, Bev. I didn't leave Rafe. He told me to get out of his life."

"And you went."

"Yes."

Bev slowly shook her head. "I won't deny that at the time I thought it was for the best."

"I can imagine your feelings on the matter. I know exactly how you felt about me as a wife for your son." Margaret smiled to cancel any bitterness that might have tinged the words. "If it makes you feel any better, I've come to agree with you."

Bev's eyes widened with sudden shock. "What are you saying?"

"That you were right when you told me I would make a lousy wife for Rafe."

"I only said that because I was afraid you would try to change him—make him into something he was not. Margaret, please believe me when I tell you that I never had anything at all against you personally. The truth is, I like you very much. I admire you." Bev smiled. "I've even started reading your books. I'm enjoying *Ruthless* enormously."

Margaret grinned. "As any author will tell you, flattery will get you anywhere. We're suckers for people who say they like our books."

"Good. Then perhaps you'll forgive me for some of the things I said to you last year?"

"We both know they were true, Bev. I would probably make Rafe very unhappy, frustrated and eventually blazingly angry if I were to marry him."

"I used to think so but I'm not so sure about that anymore, Margaret."

"I am. For starters, I would insist on our relationship getting equal billing with his business interests. Truth be known, I'd go farther than that. If the chips were down, I'd insist that our marriage come first. I would make every effort to force him to live a more balanced life. I would make him work regular hours and take vacations. And I would not play the role of the self-sacrificing executive's wife who always puts her husband's career first."

Bev sighed. "I sensed that when I met you. I think I reacted so strongly to you because I had played exactly that role for Rafe's father. I was certain Rafe needed a wife who would do the same."

"I think you're right. He does need a wife like that. But I couldn't live that life, Bev. It would turn me bitter and unhappy within a very short period of time. I want a husband who loves me more than he loves his corporation. I want a man who puts me first. I want to be the most important thing in his life. And we both know that for Rafe, business is the most important thing in the world. For him, a wife will be only a convenience."

"Margaret, listen to me. Last year I believed that every bit as much as you did. But now I no longer think that's true. Rafe has changed during the past year. Your walking out on him did that."

"I did not walk out on him."

"All right, all right, I didn't mean to put it that way." Bev held up one hand in a placating fashion. "Losing you did change him, though. I wouldn't have believed it possible if I hadn't seen it with my own eyes. Until you were gone, he was as driven to succeed as his father had been—more so because the stakes were higher after John died."

Margaret frowned. "Rafe was trying to show that he could be as successful as his father?"

"No, he was trying to rescue us from the financial disaster in which John left us." Bev's mouth tightened. "My husband was a good man in many respects, but his business was everything to him. He ate, slept and breathed Cassidy and Company. But shortly before he was killed in a plane accident, he suffered some enormous financial losses. You'll have to ask Rafe for the details. It had to do with some risky investments that went bad."

"Was Rafe involved?"

Bev shook her head. "No. Rafe had gone off on his own. He was too much like John in many ways and he knew it. He realized from the time he was in high school that he could never work for his father. They would have been constantly at each other's throats. They were both stubborn, both smart and both insisted on being in charge. An impossible working situation."

"Did your husband accept that?"

"To his credit, John did understand. He wished Rafe well when Rafe started his own business. But John always assumed that when he retired, Rafe would take over Cassidy and Company and then John was killed."

Margaret watched Bev toy with her coffee cup. "Rafe did come back to take over Cassidy and Company, then, didn't he? Just as your husband would have wanted."

"Oh, yes. Rafe took the reins. And that's when we discovered that John had been on the brink of bankruptcy. Rafe worked night and day to save the business and he did save it. Against all odds. You can be certain the financial community had already written off Cassidy and Company. We survived and the company is flourishing now, but the experience did something to Rafe."

"What do you mean?"

Bev poured more coffee. "Watching Rafe work to salvage Cassidy and Company was like watching steel being forged in fire. He went into the whole thing as a strong man or he wouldn't have survived. But he came out of it much harder, more ruthless and a lot stronger than he'd been before his experience. Too hard, too ruthless and too strong in some ways. His sister Julie calls him a gunslinger because he's made a habit of taking on all challengers."

Margaret had never met Julie. There had been no opportunity. But it sounded as if the woman had her brother pegged. She looked down into the depths of her coffee. "He didn't like losing to Moorcroft's firm last year."

"No, he did not." Bev smiled briefly. "And you can be certain that one of these days he'll find a way to even the score."

Margaret felt a frisson of uneasiness go down her spine. She thought about her conversation with Jack Moorcroft shortly before leaving Seattle. "I'm glad I'm out of it."

"What Rafe does about Moorcroft is neither here nor there. It's your relationship with my son that concerns me. Rafe put a lot of his life on hold while he worked to save Cassidy and Company. One of the things he avoided was marriage. Now he's nearly forty years old and time is running out. I think he realizes that. I want him to be happy, Margaret. I have come to realize during the past year that you are probably the one woman who can make him happy."

Margaret stared at her helplessly. "But that's just it, Bev. I can't make him happy. Not as his wife, at any rate. I simply can't be the kind of wife he wants or needs. So I'm going to take your advice."

Bev looked at her with worried eyes. "What advice?"

"I'm going to try having an affair with him."

"You mean you're not going to marry him?" Bev looked stunned.

Before Margaret could respond, her father's voice bellowed over the patio. "What the hell do you mean, you're not marrying him? Cassidy swore he was offering marriage. That's the only reason I agreed to get involved in this tomfool plan to get you down here. What the blazes does he think he's trying to pull around here?"

"Dad, hang on a minute." Margaret turned in her chair to see her father bearing down on her. "Let me explain."

"What's to explain? I'll have Cassidy's hide, by God. I'll take a horsewhip to that boy if he thinks he can lead my little girl down the garden path."

"Sit down, Dad."

Bev tried a pacifying smile. "Yes, Connor. Do sit down and let your daughter explain. You didn't hear the whole story."

"I don't need to hear anything more than the fact that Cassidy isn't proposing. That's enough for me." Connor glowered at both women, but accepted the cup Bev pushed toward him. "Don't you worry, Maggie. I'll set him straight fast enough. He'll do the right thing by you if I have to tie him up and use a branding iron on him."

Rafe came out of his bedroom at that moment, striding across the patio with his usual unconscious arrogance. Margaret watched him, memories of the night flaring again in her mind. He looked so lithe, sensual and supremely confident in a pair of jeans and a shirt that was unbuttoned at the throat. His dark hair was still damp from a shower and his eyes told her he, too, was remembering what had happened out here between them last night. When he saw he had her full attention, a slight smile edged his mouth and his left eye narrowed in a small, sexy wink.

"Morning, everyone," he said as he came to a halt beside the table. He bent his head to kiss Margaret full on the mouth and then he reached for the coffeepot. He seemed unaware of the fact that his mother was looking uneasy and that Connor was glowering at him. "Beautiful day, isn't it? When we're finished here, Maggie, love, I'll take you out to the barns and show you some of the most spectacular horseflesh you've seen in your entire life."

"Hold on there, Cassidy." Connor's bushy brows formed a solid line above his narrowed eyes. "You aren't going anywhere with my girl until we sort out a few details."

Rafe lounged back in his chair, cup in hand. "What's with you this morning, Connor? Got a problem?"

"You're the one with the problem. A big one."

"Yeah? What would that be?"

"You told me you intended to marry my Maggie. That's the only reason I overlooked the way you treated her last year and agreed to help you get her down here."

Rafe shrugged, munching on a breakfast pastry. "So?"

"So she just said you two weren't gettin' married after all."

Rafe stopped munching. His eyes slammed into Margaret's. A great deal of the indulgent good humor he had been exhibiting a minute ago had vanished from the depths of his gaze.

"The hell she did," Rafe said, his eyes still locked with Margaret's.

"Heard her myself, Cassidy, and I want some answers. Now." Connor's fist struck the table to emphasize his demand.

"You're not the only one." Rafe was still staring grimly at Margaret.

Margaret groaned and traded glances with a sympathetic-looking Bev. "You shouldn't have eavesdropped, Dad. You got it all wrong."

"I did?" Connor stared at her in confusion. "But I heard you tell Bev you and Cassidy weren't going to get married. You said something about settling for a damned affair."

"Is that right?" Rafe asked darkly. "Is that what you said, Maggie?"

Margaret got to her feet, aware of the other three watching her with unrelenting intensity. She felt cornered. "I said that I would not make a good wife for Rafe. That does not mean, however, that he and I can't enjoy an affair. I've decided to pick up where we left off last year."

"We were engaged last year," Rafe reminded her coldly.

"No, Rafe. You might have felt you were engaged because you had asked me to marry you several times, but the truth is I was still considering your proposal when everything blew up in my face. I had doubts about the wisdom of marrying you then and after having had a full year to think about it, I have even more doubts about it now. Therefore, I'm only willing to go as far as having an affair with you. Take it or leave it."

"The hell I will."

"Rafe, your mother was right. I'll make you a much better mistress than I would a wife." Without waiting for a response, Margaret turned and started toward the sanctuary of her bedroom.

She never made it. Rafe came silently up out of his chair and swooped across the patio in a few long strides. He caught her up in his arms and tossed her over his shoulder before she knew quite what had happened.

Rafe didn't pause. He didn't say a word. He simply carried her through one of the open glass doors, across the living room and out into the hot sunshine.

5

"WHAT DO YOU THINK you're doing, Rafe? This is inexcusable behavior, absolutely inexcusable. I will not tolerate it."

"It's cowboy behavior and I'm just a cowboy at heart, remember?" He strode swiftly toward one of the long, low white barns.

"You're an arrogant, high-handed bastard at heart, that's what you are." Margaret was suddenly acutely aware of an audience. Tom and another man in work clothes and boots glanced toward Rafe and grinned broadly. "Rafe, people are watching. For heaven's sake, put me down."

"I don't take orders from a mistress."

"Damn it, Rafe."

"Now, I might listen to an engaged lady or a wife, maybe, but not a mistress. No, ma'am."

"*Put me down.*"

"In a minute. I want to find us some privacy first."

"Privacy. Rafe, you're creating an embarrassing public spectacle. And you have the nerve to wonder why I never came crawling back to you on my hands and knees this past year begging you to forgive me. This sort of behavior is exactly why I considered I'd had a very lucky escape."

"Let's not bring up past history. We're supposed to be making a fresh start, remember? If I can let bygones be bygones, so can you."

"You are unbelievably arrogant."

"Yeah, but even better, I usually get what I want."

He carried her into the soft shadows of a long barn. Hanging upside-down as she was, Margaret had an excellent view of a straw-littered floor. The earthy scents of horses and hay wafted up around her. A row of equine heads with pricked ears appeared above the open stall doors.

Margaret gasped as Rafe swung her off his shoulder and onto her feet. As she regained her balance she glared at her tormentor and fumbled to readjust the clip that held her hair at her nape.

"Honestly, Rafe, that was an absolutely outrageous thing to do. I'd demand an apology but I know I won't get one. I doubt if you've ever apologized in your entire life."

"Maggie, love, we'd better have a long talk. There appears to be a slight misunderstanding here."

"Stop calling me Maggie. I've told you a hundred times I don't like it. That's another thing. You never really listen to me, do you? You think everything has to be done your way and the rest of us should just learn to like it that way, no matter what. Your mother tried to tell me this morning that you'd changed during the past year but I knew better and I was right, wasn't I? You just proved it. You're still a thickheaded, domineering, bossy, overbearing cowboy who rides roughshod over everyone else."

"That's enough." Rafe stood with his booted feet braced, his hands on his hips, his eyes narrowed dangerously.

"Good Lord, you are a real cowboy, aren't you?" Her voice was scathing. "You look right at home here in this barn with that . . . that *stuff* on your boots."

He glanced down automatically and saw the stuff to which she referred with such disdain. There was a small pile of it near his left boot. Prudently he moved the elaborately tooled black leather boot with its red and yellow star design a few inches to the right.

"Goes with the territory," Rafe said. He looked up again. "And you can quit playing the sophisticated city girl who's never seen the inside of a barn. I know the truth about you, lady. Connor and I have had a few long talks."

"Is that right?" she sniffed.

"Damned right. I know for a fact you were born on your dad's ranch in California and you were raised on it until you were thirteen. You didn't start picking up your fancy airs until Connor sold the place and your family went to live in San Francisco."

"I prefer to forget my rustic background," she retorted. "And for your information, my standards have changed since I was thirteen. For all intents and purposes, I'm very much a city girl now and I expect a certain level of appropriate behavior from the male of the species."

"You'll take the behavior you get. Furthermore, I think I've had all the squawking I want to hear from you, *city girl*. You're not the only one who expects a certain level of appropriate social behavior. You're acting like a sharp-tongued, temperamental prima donna who thinks she can play games with me."

"That's not true."

"Yeah? Then what was all that nonsense by the pool a few minutes ago? What do you think you're doing telling our folks you don't intend to marry me?"

"It's the truth. I don't intend to marry you. I've never said I would marry you. Marrying you would be an extremely dumb thing for me to do."

The glittering outrage in his eyes was unnerving. Rafe took a single step closer. Margaret took a prudent step backward. A horse in a nearby stall wickered inquiringly.

"I didn't bring you down here to set you up as a mistress and you know it," Rafe said between his teeth.

"Don't use that word."

"What word? Mistress? That's what you're suggesting we call you, isn't it?"

"No, it's not." Margaret scowled angrily. "That's your mother's word. I explained to you last night, people like her and my father come from another generation."

"You also said that deep down you didn't think we were all that different from them," Rafe shot back. "What the hell did you think you were doing last night if you weren't agreeing to come back to me?"

She lifted her chin. "Last night I decided that we might try resuming our affair."

"That's real generous of you. The only problem is that we don't happen to have an affair to resume."

She glared at him in open challenge. "Is that right? What do you call us sleeping together for nearly two months last year?"

"Anticipating our wedding vows."

Margaret stared at him, open-mouthed. She did not know whether to laugh or cry. Rafe looked perfectly serious, totally self-righteous. "You're joking. That's what you called our affair? How quaint. But there never was a wedding, so what does that make the whole business? Besides a big mistake, I mean?"

"There's damn well going to be a wedding."

"Why?" she asked bluntly.

"Because you and I belong together, that's why. And you know it, Maggie. Or have you forgotten last night already?"

"No, I haven't forgotten it, but just because we're good together in bed does not mean we should get married. Rafe, listen to me. I've tried to explain to everyone that I would make you a lousy wife. Why won't anyone pay any attention to what I'm saying?"

"Because you're talking garbage, that's why."

Margaret sighed heavily. "This is impossible. We're getting nowhere. Talk about a communication problem. I'd better leave—the sooner the better."

Rafe reached out and caught her arm as she would have turned away. A fierce determination blazed in his eyes and his voice had a raw edge to it. "You can't leave. Not now. I spent six months in hell trying to pretend you didn't exist and another six months figuring out ways to get you back. I'm not going to let you go this time."

"You can't stop me, Rafe. Oh, I know I let you coerce me into coming down here. But we both know you can't make me stay against my will. And the truth is, there's nothing I can do here, anyway. I've seen for myself that my father is happy with your mother. I would hurt him by trying to interfere. And if he wants to sell Lark Engineering to you, that's his business. It's clear you're not trying to cheat him out of the firm."

"I didn't bring you down here so that you could protect your father. We both know he can take care of himself. I got you down here so that we could start over again, Maggie, and you know it. Furthermore, if you're honest with yourself for once, you'll admit that's why you used that ticket so damn fast once I'd given you a good enough excuse."

He was right and that jolted her. She had known all along that her father could take care of himself, even against the likes of Rafe Cassidy. Everyone involved had politely let her pretend that she had rushed down here to rescue Connor but everyone knew the truth.

"This is extremely humiliating," Margaret said.

"If it makes you feel any better, take it from me you don't know what I was going through yesterday morning at the airport waiting to see if you were on that flight. I was afraid to even call your apartment in Seattle in case you answered the phone. How's that for proof that you have an equal ability to make me feel like an idiot?"

The intensity of his words shook her. She bit her lip and then reached out hesitantly to touch his hand. When he glanced down she withdrew her fingers immediately. "Rafe, it won't work. We might have managed a long-distance affair. For a while. But we'll never manage a marriage. Your mother was right all along."

"Stop saying that, damn it. She was wrong and she admits it. Why do you keep quoting something she said a year ago as if it were carved in stone?"

"Because she was right a year ago. You're a driven man when it comes to business or anything else you decide you want. This morning she told me more about why you're driven but that doesn't change anything. It just helps explain why you are the way you are."

Rafe swore in disgust. "She gave you some tripe about me being somewhat, uh, aggressive in business because I had to work so hard to rescue Cassidy and Company, didn't she? Julie says that's her current theory on my behavior."

"Well, yes. And you're not *somewhat* aggressive, Rafe, you're a real predator. What's more, you get downright hostile when someone steals your prey the way you think I helped Moorcroft do last year."

"Look, maybe I'd better make one thing clear here. My mother likes to think I'm the way I am—I mean, was—because of what happened after Dad was killed. But the truth is, I was like that long before I took over Cassidy and Company. Dad knew it. Hell, I was born that way, according to my father. Same as he was."

Margaret nodded sadly. "You didn't change so that you could salvage the company, you managed to salvage the company because you were already strong enough and aggressive enough to do it."

"But things are different now. I've changed. I keep telling you that. Give me a chance, Maggie."

"Last night I thought I could."

"You call having an affair with me giving me a chance?" he demanded incredulously.

She nodded. "It was a way to try again. A way that left us both free to change our minds without breaking any promises. It would have given us time to observe each other and reassess the situation."

"Hell." He ran his hand through his hair in a gesture of pure frustration. "I don't need any more time, Maggie. I've been reassessing this damned situation for months."

"Well, I do need time."

"This isn't just a question of my work habits, is it?" he asked shrewdly. "The truth is you aren't going to forgive me for what happened between us last year, are you?"

"You've never asked me to forgive you, Rafe." She smiled bleakly. "You're much too proud for that, aren't you? Oh, you very generously forgave me, but you don't think you need to be forgiven. It's all black and white to you. You were right and I was clearly in the wrong."

"You made a mistake. Conflicting sets of loyalties, as I said. You were under a lot of pressure at the time and you got confused."

"So confused I'd do it again if I had to. I didn't like being used, Rafe."

His jaw tightened. "I did not use you."

"That's not the way I saw it. You knew I was working for Jack Moorcroft when you started dating me, didn't you?"

"Yeah, but damn it . . ."

"I, on the other hand, did not have the advantage of knowing you were a business rival of his. I didn't even realize you two knew each other, let alone were fierce competitors. You kept that information from me, Rafe."

"Only because I knew you'd have a problem dating me in the beginning if you knew the whole truth. I didn't want to lose you by telling you Moorcroft and I were after the same prize. You'd have felt guilty going out with me. And if you'll recall, I never tried to pump you for inside information."

"You let me talk about my job," she accused. "You let me tell you about the projects I was working on. You showed so much interest in me. I was so terribly flattered by that interest. It makes me sick to think how flattered I was."

"What was I supposed to do? Tell you not to talk about your work?"

"Yes. That's exactly what you should have told me."

"Be reasonable, Maggie. If I had tried to explain just why you shouldn't talk to me about your job, you'd have very quickly figured out who I was. I couldn't let that happen."

"Because you needed the inside information in order to beat Moorcroft to Spencer."

"That's a lot of horse manure," he told her roughly. "I didn't tell you to shut up about your work because I'd have lost you if I had. If it makes you feel any better, you can rest assured I had all the information I needed to beat Moorcroft to the punch from other sources. Nothing you told me made any difference in my plans."

"Oh, Rafe."

"You want the flat honest truth? Moorcroft's the one who got the advantage out of our relationship. You ran to him that morning and warned him I was after Spencer. Thanks to you, he was able to move his timetable ahead fast enough to knock me out of the running. I was the one who lost out because I was sleeping with a woman who felt her first loyalty belonged to another man."

Margaret looked up at him appealingly, longing to believe him and knowing she should not. "Rafe, is that the full truth? Really? You didn't use any of the information I accidently gave you?"

His mouth twisted ruefully. "It's the truth, all right. If you'd known everything in the beginning, you'd have assumed I'd started dating you because of your connection to Moorcroft and you'd have backed right off. Don't try to deny it. I know you. That's exactly how your brain would have worked—exactly how it did work when you finally discovered who I was."

Margaret felt cornered again. He was right. She would have been instantly suspicious of his motives if she'd known who he was back at the beginning. "And you really didn't need inside information from me?"

"I already had most of it. Nothing you told me was particularly crucial one way or the other. In fact, if you'll stop and think about it, you'll recall that you didn't talk all that much about your job. You mostly talked about the career in writing that you were working on. I heard all your big plans to work two more years in the business world and then quit to write full-time."

"I wish I could believe that." She clasped her hands in front of her, remembering her terrible feeling of guilt at the time. "I felt like such a fool. I felt so used. I went over and over every conversation we'd had, trying to recall exactly what I'd told you. I knew I had to go straight to Moorcroft, of course. He had trusted me. I had to make up for what I'd done to him."

"You didn't do one blasted thing to him," Rafe roared. "I was the one you screwed."

She frowned in annoyance. "You don't have to be quite so crude about it."

He spread his hands in a disgusted movement and made an obvious grab for his self-control. "Forget it. I'm sorry I mentioned my side of the story. I know you aren't particularly interested in it. You're only concerned with your side."

Tears welled in Margaret's eyes. She blinked them back as she sank down onto a bale of hay and tried to think. "It was such an awful mess at the time," she whispered. "And when I tried to do the right thing by warning Moorcroft about you, you turned on me like a...a lion or something. All teeth and claws. The things you said to me... You ripped me to shreds, Rafe. I wasn't certain for a while if I was ever going to recover."

"You weren't the only one who felt ripped up." Rafe sat down beside her, elbows resting on his knees, his big hands loosely clasped. He stared straight ahead at a pretty little gray mare who was watching the proceedings with grave curiosity. "I wasn't sure I was going to make it, either." He paused for a moment. "My mother says it was probably the best thing that ever happened to me."

"She said *what*?"

"She said I needed a jolt like that to make me pay attention to something else in life besides business." His smile was ironic. "Believe me, after what happened last year, you had my full attention. I couldn't stop thinking about you no matter how hard I tried. I've put more energy into getting you back than I've ever put into a merger or a buy-out."

Margaret thought she really would cry now. "Rafe, I don't know what to say."

He turned his head, his eyes glittering with intensity. "Say you'll give me a chance, a real chance. Let's start over, Maggie. For good this time. Give me the next two weeks and be honest about it. Don't spend the time looking for excuses and a way out."

The love for him that she had been forced to acknowledge to herself last night made Margaret lightheaded. She looked into his tawny eyes and felt herself falling back into the whirlpool in which she had nearly drowned last year. "You are a very dangerous man for me, Rafe. I can't go through what I went through last time. I can't."

He caught her chin on the edge of his hand. "You're not the only one who wouldn't survive it a second time. So there won't be a second time."

She searched his eyes. "How can you be so certain?"

"Two reasons. The first is that we learned something from that fiasco. We've both changed. We aren't quite the same people we were last year."

"And the second reason?"

He smiled faintly. "You aren't working for Moorcroft or anyone else, so the pressures you had on you last time don't exist."

"But if they did exist?"

Rafe's smile hardened briefly. "This time around your commitments are clearer, aren't they? This time around you'd know your first loyalty belongs to me."

"What about *your* loyalty?" she challenged softly, knowing she was sliding deeper into the whirlpool. In another moment she would be caught and trapped.

Rafe cradled her face between two rough palms. "You are the most important person in my life, Maggie, love. My first loyalty is to you."

"Business has absolutely nothing to do with this?"

"Hell, no."

"If there were to be a conflict between our relationship and your business interests, would our relationship win?"

"Hands down."

Her fingers tightened around his wrists. Everything in her wanted to believe him. Margaret knew her future was at stake. If she had any sense she would get out while she still could.

"Rafe . . ."

"Say it, Maggie. Say you'll stay here and give me a real chance."

She closed her eyes and took a deep breath. "All right."

He groaned and pulled her close against him, his arms locking around her. His mouth moved against her sleekly knotted hair. "You won't regret it, Maggie. This time it will work. You'll see. I'll make it work. I've missed you so much, sweetheart. Last night . . ."

"What about last night?" she asked softly.

"Last night was like taking the first glass of cool water after walking out of the desert. Except that you're never cool in bed. You're hotter than the sun in August. Lord, Maggie, last night was good."

She hugged him, her head resting on his chest. "Yes."

"Maggie?"

"Um?"

"You said a few minutes ago that I'd never asked for forgiveness because I was too arrogant to think I needed it. But I'm asking for it now. I'm sorry I was so rough with you last year."

She took a breath. It was probably as much of an apology as she was likely to get. "All right, Rafe. And I'm sorry I assumed you'd been using me to beat Moorcroft. I should have known better."

"Hush, love. It's all right." His hands stroked her back soothingly. "We'll make this a fresh start. No more talk about the past."

"Agreed."

For a long while they sat on the bale of hay, saying nothing. If anyone came or went in the barn, Margaret didn't notice. She was conscious only of the feel of Rafe's hands moving gently on her. With a deep sigh of newly found peace, she gave herself up to the luxury of once more being able to nestle in Rafe's strong arms. *A fresh start.*

For the first time in a year something that had felt twisted and broken deep inside her relaxed and became whole again.

"Boss?" Tom's shout from the far end of the barn had a trace of embarrassed hesitation in it. "Hatcher's here. Says he needs to talk to you."

THE JOKER GOES WILD!

Play
this
card
right!

See
inside!

HARLEQUIN
WANTS TO <u>GIVE</u> YOU

- 4 free books
- A free gold-plated chain
- A free mystery gift

IT'S A WILD, WILD, WONDERFUL
FREE OFFER!

HERE'S WHAT YOU GET:

1. *Four New Harlequin Temptation® Novels—FREE!* Everything comes up hearts and diamonds with four exciting romances—yours FREE from Harlequin Reader Service®. Each of these brand-new novels brings you the passion and tenderness of toda greatest love stories.

2. *A Lovely and Elegant Gold-Plated Chain—FREE!* You'll love yo elegant 20k gold electroplated chain! The necklace is finely crafted with 160 double-soldered links and is electroplate finish in genuine 20k gold. And it's yours free as added thanks for givin our Reader Service a try!

3. *An Exciting Mystery Bonus—FREE!* You'll go wild over this surprise gift. It is attractive as well as practical.

4. *Free Home Delivery!* Join Harlequin Reader Service® and enjoy the convenience of previewing 4 new books every month deliver to your home. Each book is yours for $2.39—26¢ less than the cover price. And there is no extra charge for postage and handling! If you're not fully satisfied, you can cancel at any time, just by sending us a note or shipping statement marked "cancel" or by returning any shipment to us at our cost. Great savings and total convenience are the name of the game at Harlequin!

5. *Free Newsletter!* It makes you feel like a partner to the world's most popular authors...tells about their upcoming books...even gives you their recipes!

6. *More Mystery Gifts Throughout the Year!* No joke! Because hom subscribers are our most valued readers, we'll be sending you additional free gifts from time to time with your monthly shipments—as a token of our appreciation!

GO WILD
WITH HARLEQUIN TODAY—
JUST COMPLETE, DETACH AND
MAIL YOUR FREE-OFFER CARD!

IT'S NO JOKE!

MAIL THE POSTPAID CARD AND GET FREE GIFTS AND $10.60 WORTH OF HARLEQUIN NOVELS—*FREE!*

Rafe slowly released Margaret. "Tell him I'll be there in a minute."

"Right."

Rafe looked down at Margaret, his expression rueful. "Sorry about this. Hatcher's timing isn't always the best. Want to come say hello to him?"

"Okay. But he probably doesn't want to say hello to me."

"Maggie, love, you're getting paranoid. You thought my mother wouldn't want to see you again, either, but she could hardly wait for you to get down here, right? Don't worry about Hatcher's opinion. He works for me and he does what I say."

Shaking her head, Margaret let Rafe tug her to her feet. He draped an arm possessively around her shoulders and guided her out of the barn. She blinked as she stepped out into the hot sunlight. There was an unfamiliar car in the drive.

Doug Hatcher was already standing in the doorway of Rafe's home, a briefcase in one hand. Rafe's chief executive assistant looked very much as Margaret remembered him from the occasions he had accompanied his fast-moving boss to Seattle.

Hatcher was in his early thirties, a thin, sharp-faced man with pale eyes. He was dressed in a light-colored business suit, his tie knotted crisply in defiance of the heat. He did not seem surprised to see Margaret coming out of the barn with his boss.

"Good morning, Miss Lark." Hatcher inclined his head politely. "Nice to see you again."

"Thank you, Doug." She knew he was lying through his teeth. The poor man was no doubt struggling mightily to maintain a polite facade. There was little chance he was actually glad to see her. Hatcher was fiercely loyal to Rafe and he probably blamed her for the collapse of the Spencer deal last year. She was not at all certain his opinion of her would have changed just because Rafe ordered him to change it.

Then, again, when Rafe gave orders, people tended to obey.

"What's up, Hatcher?" Rafe asked easily. "I'm on vacation, remember?"

"Yes, sir." Hatcher indicated the briefcase. "I just need to update you on a couple of things. You said you wanted to keep close track of the Ellington deal. There have been a couple of recent developments I felt you should know about. I also have some figures to show you."

Rafe released Maggie abruptly. His good mood seemed to have suddenly evaporated. She recognized the signs instantly. She could almost feel him shifting gears into what she always thought of as his "business alert" mode. He was fully capable of remaining in it for hours, even days, on end. When he was caught up in it nothing else mattered to him. He brooked no distractions, not even from the woman he was currently bedding.

"Right," Rafe said. "Let's go inside and take care of it. Maggie, why don't you take a swim or something?"

Her first reaction was a rush of anger. Same old Rafe. As soon as business reared its ugly head, he was like a hunter who had caught the scent of prey. He was already dismissing her while he took care of more important things.

Then she looked at his face and saw the tension in him. He knew what she was thinking. The fact that her incipient disapproval had gotten through to him was something, she told herself. Last year he wouldn't have even noticed.

"I don't really feel like a swim, Rafe."

"Honey, this won't take long, I swear it. I guarantee I've developed some new ways of working lately but I can't just let go of everything, you know that. I'm still responsible for my family, the ranch and a heck of a lot of jobs at Cassidy and Company. Be reasonable."

She relaxed slightly as she saw the expression in his eyes. "I know, Rafe. It's all right. I understand. I think I will have that swim, after all." Of course he couldn't let go of everything. She didn't expect him to abandon his business altogether. She just wanted him to learn to put things in perspective. He was trying, she realized. And that was the first step.

Rafe nodded once, looking vastly relieved. "Thanks. Let's go, Hatcher. I want to get this over with as fast as possible. I've got other things to do today. More interesting things."

"Yes, sir."

Margaret preceded both men into the house and was turning to go down the hall to her bedroom when Bev Cassidy came through the patio doors. Connor Lark was right behind her. They both looked anxiously first at Margaret and then at Rafe.

"You two get this marriage business settled?" Connor demanded aggressively. "Bev and I aren't takin' off for Sedona day after tomorrow the way we planned if you two haven't worked this out."

"Don't worry, Connor. Everything's under control," Rafe said mildly.

"You sure?"

"I'm sure," Rafe said.

"About time."

"Yeah. You can say that again." Rafe started toward the study he used as an office. "I need to spend a few minutes with Hatcher. Maggie's going swimming, aren't you, Maggie?"

"Looks like it," said Maggie.

Bev brightened. "I've got another idea, if you're interested, Margaret?"

"What's that?" Margaret smiled.

"How would you like to go shopping? I thought you might want to buy something to wear to the engagement party tomorrow evening."

Margaret reeled. Her eyes widened in shock as she whirled to glare at Rafe. "*Engagement party.* Now, just hold on one minute, here, I've never said anything about getting officially engaged. Don't you dare try to rush me like this, Rafe. Do you hear me? I won't stand for it."

Hatcher, Conner and Bev looked at each other in obvious embarrassment. But there was a suspiciously humorous glint in Rafe's eyes when he said very gently, "Mom is talking about the engagement party she and Connor are giving tomorrow night to celebrate their engagement. Not ours."

"I'm so sorry, dear," Bev said quickly. "In all the excitement of your arrival yesterday, I forgot to mention it. We're having a few friends over to celebrate tomorrow evening. The next day Connor and I are going to take a little trip."

Margaret learned the meaning of wishing the floor would open up and swallow her whole. "Oh," she said, flushing a bright pink. She turned to Bev. "Shopping sounds like a wonderful idea. I haven't a thing to wear."

6

MARGARET PAUSED at the edge of the pool, glanced around quickly at the patio full of well-dressed guests and realized she was alone at last. When she spotted her father disappearing into the house by himself she decided to take advantage of the situation. She put down her empty hors d'oeuvres plate and hurried after him.

"Caught you, Dad." She grinned triumphantly at a startled Connor as he headed toward the kitchen.

"Maggie, my girl." Connor made an effort to look genuinely pleased to see her. "I was wonderin' how you were gettin' along. Enjoyin' yourself, girl? Bev sure knows how to throw a mighty fine party, doesn't she? One of the things I love about her. She knows how to have a good time. Wouldn't think it to look at her, but she's not a bit stuffy or prissy. Great sense of humor."

Margaret folded her arms and regarded her father with a sense of amusement mixed with exasperation. "Bev Cassidy appears to be an all-around wonderful person and I'm delighted the two of you are so happy together, but I didn't corner you in here to listen to a glowing litany of her attributes. You've been avoiding me since I got here, Dad. Admit it."

Connor appeared shocked and horrified at the accusation. "Avoidin' you? Not a chance, girl. How could you think such a thing? You're my own little Maggie, my only child, the fruit of my loins."

"Hold it, Dad."

"It's nothin' less than the truth. Hell's bells, girl, why would I want to avoid you? I'm delighted you got down here for my engagement shindig. A man's one and only child should definitely be present when he takes the great leap into marriage."

"That's arguable, depending on when the leap is made," Margaret said dryly. "But your impending nuptials, exciting as they may be, are not what I wanted to discuss."

"Maggie, girl, you know I'm always available to you. I'm your father. Your own flesh and blood. You can talk to me about anything."

"Terrific. That's just what I'd like to do. I have a little matter I've been wanting to discuss with you ever since I got here."

Connor brightened. "Wonderful. We'll have us a nice father-daughter chat one of these days just as soon as we both have a spare minute."

"I've got a spare minute right now."

"Well, shoot, too bad I don't." Connor's face twisted into a parody of sincere regret. "Promised Bev I'd get on the kitchen staff's tails. We're runnin' out of ice. Maybe sometime in the mornin'?"

"Rafe is going to take me riding in the morning, if you'll recall."

"Hey, that's right. I remember him sayin' somethin' about that earlier today. You haven't been ridin' for quite a while, have you? You used to be darn good at it. Don't worry about bein' out of practice. It's like bicyclin'. Once you get the hang of it, you never forget. Rafe's got some fine horses, doesn't he?"

"I'm sure Rafe's horses are all first class. They're a business investment and Rafe has excellent instincts when it comes to business investments. Dad, stop trying to sidetrack me. I want to talk to you."

Connor exhaled heavily, surrendering to the inevitable. He eyed Margaret warily. "More likely you want to chew me out for my part in Rafe's little plot. You still mad about that? I thought you and Rafe had settled things."

"Rafe and I have an ongoing dialogue about certain matters."

Conner wrinkled his nose. "Is that a fancy way of sayin' everything's settled?"

"It's a way of saying we're both reevaluating the situation and waiting to see how things develop."

"You know, Maggie, girl, for a woman who's made a career out of writin' romance novels, you sure do have an unexcitin' turn of phrase when it comes to describin' your own love life. *Reevaluatin' the situation*?"

Margaret smiled ruefully. "I guess it does sound a little tame. But the truth is, Dad, after last year I'm inclined to be cautious."

Connor nodded, his eyes hardening slightly. "Yeah, I can understand that. Hell, I was inclined toward a few things, myself, after I got wind of what happened."

"Like what?"

"Like murder. Damn near killed Cassidy at our first meetin' a few months back. Raked that boy over the coals somethin' fierce, I can tell you that."

"You did?" Margaret was startled. But, then, no one had seen fit to inform her of that meeting.

"Sure. You hadn't told me all that much about what had happened, remember? You just said it was over and Cassidy had said some nasty things there at the end. But I was mad as hell because I knew how much he'd hurt my girl."

Margaret drummed her fingers thoughtfully on her forearms. "Just what did Rafe say at that first meeting?"

Connor shrugged. "Not much to start. Just let me rant and rave at him and call him every name in the book. Then, when I'd calmed down, he poured me a glass of Scotch and gave me his side of the story."

"And you instantly forgave him? Figured he was the innocent party, after all?"

"Hell, no." Connor glowered at her. "You're still my daughter, Maggie. You know I'd defend you to the last ditch, no matter what."

"Thanks, Dad."

"But," Connor continued deliberately, "I was extremely interested in the other side of the story. I'd taken to Cassidy right off when you introduced us last year. You know that. Figured he was just the man for you. Don't mind sayin' I was real upset with myself to think I'd misjudged the man that badly. I was relieved to find out the situation wasn't exactly what you'd call black and white. There was a lot of gray area and after a couple of Scotches and some rational conversation I could sort of see Cassidy's point of view."

"Rafe can be very persuasive," Margaret murmured.

"And you, Maggie, girl, can be a bit high in the instep when it suits you."

"So it was all my fault, after all? Is that what you decided?"

"No, it wasn't. Don't put words in my mouth, girl. All I'm sayin' is that when I heard Cassidy's side of the tale, I did some thinkin'."

Margaret couldn't help but grin. "You mean you reevaluated the situation?"

Connor chuckled. "Somethin' like that. At any rate, when I realized Cassidy was dead serious about gettin' you back, I figured I might lend him a hand." Connor's smile broadened conspiratorially. "Then he introduced me to Bev and I knew for certain I'd help him out."

"Your father," Rafe announced from the open doorway behind Margaret, "is a man who has his priorities straight. He just wanted you and me to get ours straightened out, too."

Margaret jumped and turned her head to glance over her shoulder. Rafe sauntered into the room, a drink in his hand. He was dressed for the party in a pair of gray, Western-cut trousers, a black shirt and a bolo tie made of white leather. His boots were also made of white leather with an elaborate floral design picked out in silver and black.

"How long have you been standing there?" Margaret asked, thinking that there were times when she felt distinctly underdressed around Rafe.

"Not long." He put his arm around her waist and grinned at Connor. "I wondered when she'd cut you out of the herd and demand a few private explanations, Connor. Need any help?"

"Nope. Maggie and I got it all sorted out, didn't we, girl?"

"If you say so, Dad."

Rafe grinned. "Good. Now that you two have that settled maybe you can give me some advice on what to do about Julie's artist friend. Did you meet him yet?" He shook his head. "I knew when she went to work managing that art supply store she'd be mixing with a bad crowd."

Margaret glared at him. "I met Sean Winters earlier this evening when I was first introduced to your sister. I like him. He seems very nice and he treats Julie like a queen. Where's the problem?"

Rafe gave her a sidelong glance as he took a swallow out of his glass. "Weren't you listening? The problem is that the guy's an artist."

"So?" Margaret arched her brows. "I'm a writer. You got something against people who make their living in the creative fields, Cassidy?"

Rafe winced. "Now, Maggie, love, don't take what I said as a personal comment, okay? I just can't see my sister marrying some guy who makes a living painting pictures."

"Why not?"

"Well, for one thing, it's not exactly a stable profession, is it? No regular salary, no benefits, no pension plan, no telling how long the career will last."

"Same with writing," Margaret assured him cheerfully. "And what's so all-fired safe about other professions? A person is always at risk of getting fired or being laid off or of being forced to resign. Look at my situation last year."

"Let's not get into that," Rafe said tersely.

"Nevertheless, you have to admit no job is really guaranteed for life. How many times have you seen a so-called friendly merger result in a purge of management that cost dozens of jobs?"

"Yeah, but . . ."

"I wouldn't be surprised if some of the mergers and buy-outs you've instigated have resulted in exactly that kind of purge."

"We're not talking about me, here, remember? We're discussing Julie's artist friend. Hell, he's from a whole different world. They've got nothing in common. Julie's got a degree in business administration, although she has yet to do much with it. She's not the artsy-craftsy type. What does she see in Winters?"

"You're just looking for excuses, Rafe. You've got a typical redneck macho male's built-in prejudice against men in the creative arts and you're using the insecurity of the business as a reason to disapprove of Sean as a boyfriend for your sister."

"Damn." Rafe looked appealingly at Connor. "Wish I'd kept my mouth shut."

"Don't look to me for backup on this one." Connor gave his host a wide grin. "I learned my lesson a few years back when Maggie here was dating an artist. I tried to give her the same lecture. Couldn't see my girl getting involved with some weirdo who hung out with the art crowd. You should have seen his stuff, Cassidy. Little bits of aluminum cans stuck all over his canvasses."

That got a quick scowl out of Rafe. He glanced at Maggie. "How long did you date the weirdo?"

"Jon was not a weirdo. He was a very successful multimedia artist who has since gone on to make more from a single painting than I make from a single book. I've got one of his early works hanging in my living room, if you will recall."

Rafe's eyes narrowed. "That thing on your wall that looks like a collection of recycled junk?"

"I'll have you know that if I ever get desperate financially I'll be able to hock that collection of recycled junk for enough money to live on for a couple of years. It was a terrific investment."

"How long did you date him?" Rafe demanded again.

"Jealous?"

"Damn right."

Margaret grinned. "Don't be. Jon was a wonderful man in many respects but it was obvious from the start we weren't meant for each other."

"Yeah? How was it so obvious?"

"He was a night person. I'm a morning person. And never the twain shall meet. At least not for long."

"Glad to hear it."

"The point is, our incompatibility had nothing to do with his profession. And you shouldn't judge your sister's boyfriend on his choice of careers. Besides, Julie's old enough to make her own decisions when it comes to men."

"That's another point. He's too old for her."

"He is not. He's thirty-five. The difference between their ages isn't much more than the difference between our ages, Rafe."

"Okay, okay, let's drop this discussion. We're supposed to be celebrating an engagement here tonight." Rafe looked at Connor with a hint of desperation. "Need some help with the ice?"

"Appreciate it," Connor said.

Rafe gave Margaret a quick, hard kiss. "See you outside in a few minutes, honey."

"Go ahead. Make your escape. But keep in mind what I said about giving Sean Winters a chance." Margaret fixed both men with a meaningful glance before she turned and headed for the door.

"Whew." Rafe exhaled on a sigh of relief as he watched her leave the room. He stared after her departing figure for a moment, enjoying the sight of her neatly rounded derriere moving gently under her elegant cream silk skirt.

"I know what you mean," Connor said. "Women get funny notions sometimes. Maggie tends to be real opinionated."

Rafe took another sip of his Scotch. "Was she really torn up after she stopped seeing the artist?"

Connor laughed and started for the kitchen. "Let me put it this way. One week after she'd stopped dating him she was dating a banker. One week after you and she broke up, she went into hibernation."

Rafe nodded, satisfied. "Yeah, I know. If it makes you feel any better, Connor, my social life followed roughly the same pattern during the past year."

"That's one of the reasons I agreed to help you get her back," Connor said. "Couldn't stand to see the two of you sufferin' like a couple of stranded calves. It was pitiful, just pitiful."

"Thanks, Lark. You're one of nature's noblemen."

OUTSIDE ON THE PATIO Margaret helped herself to another round of salad while she chatted easily with several of the guests. She was answering a barrage of questions concerning publishing when Rafe's sister materialized with her friend the artist in tow.

Margaret had met Julie and Sean earlier in the evening and had liked them both although she had sensed a certain reserve in Julie. Rafe's sister was a pretty creature with light brown hair, her mother's delicate bone structure and dark, intelligent eyes.

Sean Winters was a tall, thin man who had an easygoing smile and quick, expressive features. He greeted Margaret with a smile.

"How's it going, Margaret? Cassidy find you? He was looking for you a few minutes ago," Sean said.

"He found me. He's inside helping my father with the ice. It's a lovely party, isn't it?"

"Well, hardly the sort of bash we weird, bohemian types usually enjoy. No kinky sex, funny cigarettes or heavy metal music, but I'm adjusting," Sean said.

Margaret laughed but Julie looked stricken.

"Don't say that," Julie whispered tightly.

Sean shrugged. "Honey, it's no secret your brother isn't all that enthusiastic about having an artist in the family."

Julie bit her lip. "Well, he's going to have one in the family, so he better get used to the idea. I won't have him insulting you."

"He didn't insult me. He just doesn't think I'm good enough for you."

"He's tried to play the role of father for me ever since Dad died," Julie explained apologetically. "I know he means well, but the trouble with Rafe is that he doesn't know when to step back and let someone make their own decisions. He's been giving orders around here so long, he assumes that's the way the world works. Rafe Cassidy says jump and everyone asks how high. He's totally astounded when someone doesn't." Julie glanced at Margaret. "The way Margaret didn't last year."

"I don't know what you mean," Margaret said calmly. "I followed orders last year. Rafe said to get out and I went."

Julie sighed. "Yes, but you were supposed to come back."

"So I've been told. On my hands and knees."

"Would that have been so hard?"

"Impossible," Margaret assured her, aware of the sudden tightness in her voice. Her pride was all she'd had left last year. She'd clung to it as if it had been a lifeline.

"My brother was in bad shape for a long time after you left. I've never seen him the way he was this past year and I admit I blamed you for it. I think I hated you myself for a while, even though I'd never met you. I couldn't stand what you'd done to him." Julie's dark eyes were very intent and serious.

Margaret understood the reserve she'd sensed in Rafe's sister. "It's natural that you'd feel protective of your brother."

"It was a battle of wills as far as Rafe was concerned. And he lost. He doesn't like to lose, Margaret."

Margaret blinked. "He lost? How on earth do you figure that?"

"He finally realized that the only way you were going to come back was for him to lower his pride and go and get you. It was probably one of the hardest things he's ever done. Mom says now that it was good for him, but I'm not so sure."

"Lower his pride?" Margaret was flabbergasted by that interpretation of events. "You think that's what Rafe did when he went to Seattle to fetch me down here?"

"Of course."

"Julie, it wasn't anything like that at all. Not that it's anyone else's business, but the truth is, I was virtually blackmailed and kidnapped. I didn't notice Rafe having to surrender one square inch of his pride."

"Then you don't know my brother very well," Julie said. She put her hand on Sean's arm. "But I shouldn't say anything. It's between you and Rafe. Mom may have been right, maybe Rafe did need the jolt you gave him. He's accustomed to having things his way and it's no secret that people cater to him. But that doesn't change the fact that he's human and he can be hurt. And he's got a thing about loyalty."

"I don't think you need to worry about protecting your big brother," Sean murmured. "Something tells me he can take care of himself."

Julie groaned. "You're right. Besides, right now I've got my own problems with him. To tell you the truth, Margaret, I'm inclined to sympathize with you at the moment. Rafe can be extremely bullheaded when it comes to his own opinions. I haven't dared tell him yet just how serious Sean and I are. He thinks we're just dating casually, but the truth is Sean and I are going to get married whether Rafe approves or not."

"Give Rafe a chance to know Sean." Margaret smiled at the artist. "He's really fairly reasonable about most things, once you get his full attention."

"If you say so."

"I'm sure you know as well as I do that folks in the business world have a hard time understanding people in the art world."

"True." Sean's eyes gleamed with amusement. "And the situation isn't improved any by the fact that Cassidy is basically a cowboy who happens to be a genius when it comes to business. Maybe I should invite him to a showing of some of my work. Then he could at least judge me on the basis of my art. If he's going to criticize me, he might as well know what he's talking about."

"But Rafe hates modern art," Julie exclaimed.

"He's fully capable of appreciating it if he puts his mind to it," Margaret said. She remembered the discussion she'd had with Rafe on good wine and good hotels. "He may be a cowboy at heart, but he's very good at moving in different worlds when he feels like it."

Julie eyed her thoughtfully. "You've got a point. My brother likes to play the redneck when it suits him, but I've heard him talk European politics with businessmen from England and West Germany and I've even seen him eat sushi with some Japanese distributors."

Margaret looked up at Sean. "Letting him see your work is not a bad idea at all, Sean. When's the next scheduled exhibition of your work?"

Julie interrupted before Sean could reply. "There's one on Monday evening at the gallery here in town that handles Sean's work. Do you think you could convince Rafe to come?"

"I'll talk to him," Margaret promised.

"Don't get your hopes up, Julie." Sean's voice was gentle. "Even if Margaret gets him there we can't expect him to instantly change his mind about me."

"No," Julie agreed, "but it would at least be a sign that he's willing to give you a chance. Margaret, if you can pull this off, I will definitely owe you one."

Margaret laughed, feeling completely relaxed around Julie for the first time since she had met her. "I'll keep that in mind."

Julie turned to Sean. "Look, the band is starting up again. Let's dance."

"All right. I could use a few more lessons in Western swing. If I'm going to marry a ranch girl, I'd better learn a few of the ropes." Sean put down his glass. He nodded at Margaret. "Thanks," he said as he took Julie's arm.

"No problem. Us non-business types sometimes have to stick together."

"You've got a point."

Margaret watched the handsome couple disappear into the throng of people dancing on the patio. She was idly tapping her foot and wondering where Rafe was when she suddenly became aware of Doug Hatcher standing behind her. She turned to smile brightly at him, thinking that he was about to ask her to dance. But his first remark dispelled that illusion.

"You're settling in very quickly around here, aren't you?" Doug's words were carefully enunciated, as if he was afraid of slurring them.

Margaret felt a frisson of uneasiness. "Hello, Doug. I didn't see you there. Enjoying the party?" She eyed the half-empty glass in his hand and the careful way he was holding himself and wondered if he was a little drunk. She realized she had never before seen him drink anything at all.

"You've definitely moved in on the Cassidy clan." Doug took a long pull on his drink. "You're changing things around here."

"I am?"

"Don't be so modest, Miss Lark." Doug stared at her and nodded, as if at some private understanding. "Yeah. You've changed him all right."

"Are we talking about Rafe?"

"He's different now."

"In what way, Doug?"

"Getting soft."

"*Soft?* Rafe?" She was genuinely startled by that comment.

"It's true." Doug nodded again, frowning. "When I first went to work for him he was like a knife. He'd just cut through everything in his path. But a year ago things changed. Oh, we put together a couple of good deals this past year, but it's not like the old days. I thought it was going to be all right for the first few months but then he decided he wanted you back."

"He talked about me to you?"

Doug shook his head, the gesture slightly exaggerated. "He didn't have to. I know him. I knew what he was thinking about and it wasn't about business. Like I said, he's gone soft, lost his edge. When he does think about business, he only thinks about one thing these days." He turned abruptly, caught himself as he nearly lost his balance and then vanished into the crowd.

Margaret took a deep breath as she dared to hope that the one thing Rafe thought about most these days was her. She didn't expect him to spend the rest of his life focusing entirely on her, she told herself. She fully understood that he had a major corporation to run and a ranch to manage. She had no intention of being unreasonable.

But it was comforting to know that there was growing evidence that she was finally important enough to him to make him alter his normal way of doing business. A year ago she had not been at all certain she held that much significance in his life.

"You look like you're enjoying yourself, Maggie, love." Rafe materialized out of the crowd and took her hand to lead her onto the dance floor. "Can I conclude that the thought of engagement parties in general no longer is enough to send you running for cover?"

She smiled up at him, aware of the sheer pleasure of being in his arms. His beautifully controlled physical strength was one of the most compelling qualities he possessed. She loved being wrapped up in it. "I'm having a great time at this one," she admitted.

"One of these days we'll start planning another one."

His certainty always left her feeling breathless. "Will we?"

"Yeah, Maggie, love. We will."

"I thought I was going to get plenty of time to make up my mind."

"I promised you a little time to get used to the idea of marrying me, but don't expect me to give you an unlimited amount of rope. Knowing you, you'd just get yourself all tangled up in it."

She shook her head in wry wonder. "You are always so sure of yourself, aren't you?"

"I am when I know what I want." Rafe came to a halt in the middle of the dance floor. "And now, if you'll excuse me, it's time to make the big announcement. I've been assigned to do the honors."

"Doesn't it seem a little odd that you're announcing your own mother's engagement?"

"We live in interesting times." He kissed her forehead. "Be back in a few minutes."

The crowd broke into loud applause and cheers as Rafe grabbed a bottle of champagne, vaulted up onto the diving board and strode out to the far end. He held up the bottle in his hand to get the crowd's attention.

"You all know why you're here tonight, but I've been told to make it official," he began with a grin. "I would therefore like to say that it gives me great pleasure to do as my Mama tells me and announce her engagement to one smooth-talking cowboy named Connor Lark."

A roar of approval went up. Rafe gave the crowd a couple of minutes to grow quiet once more before he continued.

"I'm here to tell you folks that I've got no choice but to approve of this match. It's not just because I've had Lark checked out and decided he can take care of my

Mama in the style to which she has become accustomed—"

The crowd interrupted with a burst of applause.

"And it's not just because she seems to actually like the guy or the fact that he's crazy about her. No, folks, I am giving my heartfelt approval to this match because Lark has informed me that if I do not, he will personally drag me out into the desert and stake me out over an anthill. Folks, I am a reasonable man. I want you to know I can hardly wait for Connor Lark to marry my mother."

Laughter filled the air as Rafe let the cork out of the champagne bottle with a suitable explosion. Again the crowd yelled approval. Connor, standing at the side of the pool next to Bev, grinned broadly at Rafe as he held a glass up to be filled with bubbling champagne.

Rafe filled the glass with a flourish and then a second one for his mother and everyone toasted the guests of honor. Connor finished his drink in one swallow and kissed his fiancée. Then he gave a whoop and grabbed her hand.

"Honey, let's dance," Connor crowed, sweeping Bev into a waltz. She laughed up at him with undisguised delight.

"They make a great couple, don't they?" Rafe leaped lightly down from the diving board and went to stand beside Margaret. He put an arm around her shoulder and drew her close to his side.

"Yes," Margaret said, her eyes on her father's face. "They do. I think they're going to be very happy."

"No happier than you and me, Maggie, love, you'll see." Rafe kissed her soundly and then dragged her over to the section of the patio that was being used for dancing. He smiled down into her eyes as he whirled her into the Western waltz.

A moment later the patio was filled with dancing couples and Margaret gave herself up to the joy of the music that flowed around her like champagne. *Yes*, she allowed herself to think for the first time in a year, *yes, she could be very happy with Rafe*. She could be the happiest woman in the world.

RAFE SAW HATCHER HANGING back as the last of the guests took their leave. He scowled at his assistant, wondering if Doug had followed orders two hours go and laid off the booze.

"You sober enough to get behind the wheel, Hatcher?" he asked bluntly as the two men stood isolated on one side of the front drive.

"I'm fine," Hatcher muttered. "Haven't had anything but soda for the past couple of hours. Just wanted to tell you I left the Ellington file in your study. You'd better take a look at it as soon as possible."

Rafe eyed him. "Something new come up?"

Hatcher nodded, his eyes sliding away to follow the last car out of the drive. "Today. I've updated the file so you can take a look for yourself. I didn't want to say anything before the party. Seemed a shame to ruin it for you."

"Since when have I ever asked you to shield me from bad news? That's not what I pay you to do and you know it."

Hatcher's jaw tightened. "I know, but this is different, Rafe."

"What am I going to be looking at when I open the file?"

Hatcher hesitated. "The possibility that we've got a leak."

"Damn it to hell. You sure?"

"No, not entirely. Could be a coincidence that Moorcroft came up with the numbers he did today, but we've got to look at the other possibility."

"Someone gave him the information."

"Maybe."

"Yeah, maybe." Rafe watched the last set of taillights disappear down his long drive. "I thought we had this airtight, Hatcher."

"I thought we did, too."

"When I find out who's selling me out, I'll do a little bloodletting. Hope whoever it is realizes what he's risking."

"We don't know for sure yet, Rafe," Hatcher said quickly. "It really could be a genuine coincidence. But regardless of how it happened, there's no getting around the fact that we've got to counter Moorcroft's last move and fast. Thought you'd want to run the numbers yourself."

"I'll do it tonight and have an answer in the morning. Nothing gets in the way of this Ellington thing, understand? It has to go through on schedule."

"Right, well, guess I'd better be off." Hatcher nodded once more and dug his keys out of his pocket. "I'll talk to you tomorrow."

Rafe stood for a while in the balmy darkness watching Hatcher's car vanish in the distance.

Vengeance was a curious thing, he acknowledged. It had the same ability to obsess a man's soul as love did.

"Rafe?"

He turned toward the sound of Maggie's soft, questioning voice. She looked so beautiful standing there in the doorway with the lights of the house behind her. His beautiful, proud Maggie. He needed her more than the desert needed the fierce storms of late summer. Without her, he was an empty man.

And if she ever realized what he was going to do to Moorcroft, she'd be furious. There was even a possibility she'd try to run from him again. He had to be careful, Rafe told himself. This was between him and Moorcroft, anyway. A little matter of vengeance and honor that had to be settled properly.

"I'm coming, Maggie, love." He started toward the doorway. "Mom and Dad still out waltzing by the pool?"

Margaret laughed. "Without a band? No, I think they gave up the waltzing in favor of getting some sleep before leaving for Sedona in the morning."

"Not a bad idea," Rafe said.

"What?"

"Sleep. I could use some myself and so could you. Good night, Maggie, love." He pulled her into his arms and kissed her.

Forty minutes later he watched from the other side of the patio as Margaret's light went out. For a short time he toyed with the idea of going to her room.

But the file waiting in his office was too important to ignore. He'd told Hatcher he'd have an answer by tomorrow morning.

7

MARGARET FOUND SLEEP IMPOSSIBLE. She tossed and turned, listening to the small night sounds that drifted through her window. Her mind was not cluttered with the bright images of the successful party or thoughts of her father and his new love. She wasn't thinking about any of the many things that could have been keeping her awake.

All she could think about was Julie Cassidy's remark concerning Rafe having overcome his hawklike pride in order to find a way to get Margaret back.

The notion of Rafe Cassidy lowering his pride for a woman was literally stunning.

Margaret stared up at the ceiling and realized she had never considered the events of the past few days in those terms. She had felt manipulated at first and there was no denying that to a great extent she had been.

But what had it cost Rafe to admit to himself and everyone else that he wanted her back?

She thought of all the times during those first few months after the disaster when she had almost picked up the phone and called him. Her own pride had stood in her way every time. She had nothing for which to apologize, she kept telling herself. She had done nothing wrong. She had tried to explain her side of the situation to Rafe and he had flatly refused to listen.

And then he had said terrible things to her, things that still had the power to make her weep if she summoned them to the surface of her consciousness.

No, she could never have made the call begging him to take her back and give her another chance. It would have meant sacrificing all of her pride and her sense of self-worth. Any man who required such an act of contrition was not worth having.

But it was a novelty to think that in some fashion Rafe's apparently high-handed actions lately bespoke a lowering of his own pride. Margaret realized she had never thought of it in that light.

It was true he had not actually admitted that he had been wrong last year. Other than to apologize grudgingly for his rough treatment of her, he had basically stuck to his belief that she was the one who was guilty of betrayal; the one who required forgiveness.

But there was also no denying that he was the one who had finally found a way to get them back together.

Of course, Margaret told herself, somewhat amused, being Rafe, he had found a way to do it that had not required an abject plea from him. Nevertheless, he had done it. They were back together, at least for now, and Rafe was talking about marriage as seriously as ever.

What's more, he really did seem to have changed. He was definitely making an effort to limit his attention to business. The Rafe she had seen so far this week was a different man than the one she had known last year in that respect. The old Rafe would never have taken the time to get so completely involved in organizing his mother's engagement party. Nor would he have spent as much time entertaining a recalcitrant lover.

Lover.

The word hovered in Margaret's mind. Whatever else he was, Rafe was indisputably the lover of her dreams.

She had missed being with him last night. She and Bev had sat up talking until very late and then retired. Margaret had toyed with the notion of waiting until the lights were out and then gliding across the patio to Rafe's room. But when she had finally glanced out into the darkness she had seen the two familiar figures splashing softly in the pool and quickly changed her mind. Her father and Bev had already commandeered the patio for a late-night tryst.

But tonight the patio was empty. Margaret pushed back the sheet and got out of bed. A glance across the patio showed that Rafe's room was dark. She smiled to herself as she imagined Rafe's reaction if she were to go to his bedroom and awaken him.

In her mind she visualized him sleeping nude in the snowy sheets. He would be on his stomach, his strong, broad shoulders beautifully contoured with moonlight. When he became aware of her presence he would roll onto his back, reach up and pull her down on top of him. He would become hard with arousal almost instantly, the way he always did when he sensed she wanted him. And she would ache with the familiar longing.

Margaret hesitated no longer. She put on the new gauzy cotton dress she had purchased while shopping with Bev and slid her feet into a pair of sandals. Then she went out into the night.

When she reached the other side of the patio it took her a few seconds to realize that Rafe was not in his room. She let herself inside and saw that the bed had never been turned down. Curious, she walked through into the hall.

The eerie glow under the study door caught her eye at once. An odd sense of guilt shafted through her. The poor man, she thought suddenly. Was this how he was accomplishing the job of proving he could love her and run a business at the same time? Had he been working nights ever since she got here?

She crossed the hall on silent feet and opened the door. The otherworldly light of the computer screen was the only illumination in the room. Rafe was bathed in it as he lounged in his chair, his booted feet propped on his desk. He had not changed since the party but his shirt was unbuttoned and his sleeves rolled up to his elbows. His dark hair was tousled.

There was a file lying on the desk in front of him and a spreadsheet on the computer screen. He turned his head as he heard the door open softly. In the electronic glow the hard lines of his face seemed grimmer than usual.

Margaret lounged in the doorway and smiled. "I know you think I'm a demanding woman, but I'm not this demanding. Honest."

"What's that supposed to mean?" Rafe casually closed the file in front of him and dropped it into a drawer.

"Just that when I said I wanted our relationship to get a little more attention than your work, I didn't mean you had to resort to sneaking around in the middle of the night in order to spend some time on the job. I do understand the realities of normal business, Rafe. I worked in that world for several years, remember?"

Rafe's mouth curved faintly. "Believe me, Maggie, love, our relationship has had my full attention lately. This—" he gestured at the computer screen "—was just something Hatcher wanted me to look at. I didn't feel like sleeping yet so I thought I'd take care of it tonight." He swung his feet to the floor and punched a couple of keys on the computer. He stood up as the screen went blank. "How did you find me?"

Margaret smiled into the shadows as he walked toward her. "I refuse to answer that on the grounds that you'll think I'm fast."

His laugh was soft and sexy in the darkness. "As far as I'm concerned, you could never be too fast for me, lady, not as long as I'm the one you're chasing." He stopped in front of her and drew a finger down the side of her throat to the curve of her shoulder. He smiled knowingly as he felt her answering shiver of awareness. "You went to my bedroom, didn't you?"

"Uh-huh. You weren't there."

"So you went looking. Good. That's the way it should be." He kissed her lightly on the tip of her nose and then brushed his mouth across hers. His voice deepened abruptly. "Promise me you'll always come looking for me. No matter what happens. Don't run away from me again, Maggie, love."

She touched the side of his cheek. "Not even if you send me away?"

"I was a fool. I won't make that mistake again. I learned my lesson the hard way. Promise me, Maggie.

Swear it. Say you won't leave even if things get rough between us again. Fight with me, yell at me, slam a few doors, kick me in the rear, but don't leave."

She caught her breath and then, in a soft, reckless little rush she gave him the words he wanted to hear. "I won't leave."

He groaned thickly and gathered her so tightly against him that Maggie could hardly breathe. She didn't mind. She felt his lips in her hair and then his fingers were moving up her back to the nape of her neck and into her loosened hair.

She wrapped her arms around his waist and inhaled the sensual, masculine scent of him. She kissed his chest where the black shirt was open and felt him shudder.

"Maggie, love, you feel so good."

Rafe moved backward a couple of steps and sank down into his chair. He eased Maggie up against the desk in front of him until she could feel the wooden edge along the backs of her thighs. His hands went to her legs.

"Rafe, wait, we can't. Not here, like this." She stifled a tiny laugh that was part anxiety at the thought of getting caught making love in his study and part joyous arousal.

"Why not here?"

"What if someone hears us?"

"What if they do?" He pushed the gauzy cotton hem of the dress up above her knees. Then he deliberately parted her legs with his hands and kissed the sensitive skin of her upper thigh. "Anyone with half a brain who might happen to overhear us should have enough sense to ignore us."

"Yes, but." Maggie shivered delicately as she felt his mouth on the inside of her leg. His hands had lifted the skirt of the dress up to her waist. She heard him laugh softly as he realized she was naked under the cotton shift.

"Ah, Maggie, love, I see you dressed for the occasion."

"You're a lecherous rake, Rafe Cassidy."

"No ma'am, just a simple cowboy with simple tastes. There's nothing I like better than taking a moonlight ride with you."

"A moonlight ride? Is that what you call it?"

"Yeah. You know something? I like you best when you're stark naked." He leaned forward again in the chair and dipped his tongue into the small depression in her stomach. Then his lips worked their way downward into the tight curls below her waist.

"Rafe. *Rafe*." Maggie's hands clenched his shoulders. She felt unbelievably wanton and gloriously sexy as she stood there in front of him legs braced apart by his strong hands. Her head was tipped back, her hair cascading behind her. She closed her eyes as his kisses became overwhelmingly intimate.

"So good. Sweet and sexy and so hot already." Rafe eased a finger into her.

Margaret tightened instantly and cried out softly. She could hardly stand now. She leaned back against the desk, letting it support her weight. Rafe's fingers stretched her gently and she dug her nails into his shoulders.

"That's it, Maggie, love. Let me know how it feels. Tell me, sweetheart."

"You already know what you can do to me," she whispered in between gasps of pleasure.

"Yeah, but I like to hear about it." His eyes gleamed in the darkness as he looked up into her face.

"Why?"

"You know why. It makes me crazy."

She half laughed and half groaned and tangled her fingers in his hair. "You make *me* go crazy, Rafe. Absolutely wild. I don't even feel like myself when you touch me like this."

"Good." He stood up slowly, his hands gliding along her hips and then her waist and above her breasts. He carried the cotton dress along with the movement, lifting it up over her head. When it was free, he tossed it heedlessly onto the floor.

Margaret had one last burst of sanity. "Your room. Just across the hall. We can . . ."

"No. I like you just fine where you are." He stood between her legs and lifted her up so that she was sitting on the desk. She reached back to brace herself with her hands as his mouth moved on her shoulders and traveled down to her swollen breasts.

Rafe's fingers went to the waistband of his pants. A moment later Margaret heard the rasp of his zipper.

"Aren't you going to at least take off your boots?" Margaret demanded in a husky whisper.

"No need. This'll work just fine."

She look down and saw that it would work just fine. "But what about . . . about the protection you always use?"

"Got it right here." He reached into his back pocket.

Margaret heard the soft sound of the little packet being opened. "You carry that on you?" she gasped.

"Every minute since the day you arrived. I want to be able to make love to you anywhere, anytime."

"Good heavens, Rafe." She giggled, feeling more daring and wanton than ever. "Isn't there something a bit scandalous about doing it like this—on top of a desk? With your boots on?"

"This is my office, let me run the show, okay?" He caught one nipple lightly between his teeth.

Margaret inhaled sharply. "Yes. By all means, go ahead. Run the show. Please." She sighed in surrender and ceased worrying about decorum.

Rafe eased her down until she lay across the desk in a blatantly sensual pose. Her legs hung over the edge, open and inviting. She shuddered as he moved closer.

Margaret looked up through slitted eyes as Rafe probed her tenderly with his thumbs and then slowly fitted himself to her. She felt the excitement pounding in her veins and wondered at the magic between them. It was always like this. When Rafe made love to her he took her into a different world, one where she was wild and free and deliciously uninhibited—one where she knew she was temporarily, at least, the center of his universe.

Margaret clutched at Rafe as he surged slowly, deeply into her. She tightened her legs around him as he braced himself above her, his hands planted flat on either side of her.

"Maggie, love. *Maggie.* You're so sweet and tight and, oh, sweetheart I do love the feel of you. Incredible."

She watched the hard, impassioned lines of his face as he drove into her until she could no longer concentrate on anything except the tide of excitement pooling deep within her. She closed her eyes again, lifting herself against the driving thrusts and then she felt Rafe ease one hand between their bodies.

He touched her with exquisite care and Margaret lost her breath. Her body tightened in a deep spasm and then relaxed in slow shivers that brought an intense pleasure to every nerve ending.

"*Rafe.*"

"Yes, love. Yes." And then he imbedded himself to the hilt within her. His lips drew back across his teeth as he fought to control a shout of sensual triumph and release. A moment later he dropped back into the chair behind him and dragged Margaret down onto his lap.

Margaret huddled against him, aware of his open zipper scratching her bare thigh. Rafe's hand slid slowly, absently along her leg and up to her waist. His head was pillowed against the back of his chair, his eyes closed.

"You are one wild and wicked lady," Rafe said without opening his eyes. "Imagine just walking in here bold as you please in the middle of the night when I'm trying to work and seducing me on my office desk."

Margaret smiled to herself as a thought struck her. "You know something, Rafe?"

"What?" He still seemed disinclined to move.

"I couldn't have done that last year when we were together."

He opened one eye. "Couldn't have done what? Walked into my office and seduced me? You're wrong. I'm a sucker for you. I always was."

She shook her head. "No you weren't. We always made love on your schedule and when you were in the middle of some business matter I always had to wait until you were finished. I could never have interrupted you the way I did tonight and expected you to shut down the computer so that we could make love in the middle of your office. Last year if I'd tried anything like that you'd have patted me on the head and told me to go wait in the bedroom until you finished working."

"Are you sure?"

Margaret lifted her head and glared at him. She saw the laughter in his eyes. "Of course, I'm sure. I have an excellent memory."

"I must have been a complete idiot last year. I can't imagine ignoring you if you'd traipsed into my office wearing that light little cotton thing with nothing on underneath. You know what I think?"

"What?"

"I don't think you'd have even tried it last year. You'd have waited very politely until I was finished. Maybe a little too politely. You were a very self-controlled, very restrained little executive lady last year. Cool, sleek and quite proper. I think the career in romance writing has been good for you. It's made you more inclined to make demands on me."

"You think that's good?" Margaret was startled.

Rafe sighed, his eyes turning serious in the shadows. "I think it's probably necessary. You're right when you called me arrogant and bossy and tyrannical."

"You admit it?"

"I admit it. I'm used to running things, honey. I've been giving orders so long it comes naturally. I'm also used to putting work first. My father always did and there's no denying I was following in his footsteps. Mom let him get away with doing that. But somehow, I don't think you'll let me get away with it."

"And you don't mind?"

Rafe smiled slowly. "Let's just say I'm capable of adapting."

"It's not that I'm completely insensitive to the demands you face, Rafe, you must know that," Margaret assured him earnestly. "I spent enough time in the business world to know that certain things have to be done and certain deadlines have to be met. But I don't want your work to rule our lives totally the way it did last year."

He drew his fingers through her tangled hair. In the shadows his eyes were very dark and deep. "It won't, Maggie. And if it ever threatens to, you know what you can do about it."

She grinned in delight. "Walk into your office and seduce you?"

"My door is always open to you, Maggie, love." Rafe kissed her lightly on the mouth and gave her a small nudge.

"I'm being kicked out already?" Margaret reluctantly got to her feet and reached for her cotton shift.

"Nope. We're both going to retire for the night. It's late and you and I are going to get up early to see Mom and Connor off to Sedona, remember?"

Margaret yawned. "Vaguely. Going to walk me back to my room?"

"You're the one whose sense of propriety insists that you wake up alone as long as the parents are around. If I had my way, I'd just walk you back across the hall to my room."

"Going to sneak back here and work on the computer after you've tucked me in?"

Rafe shook his head as he led her back across the hall, through his bedroom and out into the moonlit patio. "No, I saw all I needed to see. I've got an answer for Hatcher."

"It's very sweet of you to not make a fuss about letting me spend the night in my own bed, Rafe."

"Anything for you, Maggie, love. Besides, things will be different when we have the house to ourselves, won't they? I'm a patient man."

Much later Margaret awakened briefly. She automatically glanced through the glass door and followed the shaft of moonlight that struck full into Rafe's bedroom. She couldn't be positive, but it looked as if his bed was still empty.

CONNOR AND BEV TOOK their leave immediately after breakfast the next morning. Margaret stood with Bev in the driveway as the last of the luggage was loaded into the car.

"We'll be gone about a week, dear," Bev said cheerfully. "We're going to stop in Scottsdale first. That's where I live most of the time now. This ranch is a little too isolated for my tastes. At any rate, I have some friends I want Connor to meet. And then we'll drive on to Sedona. It makes a nice break this time of year. Much cooler up there in the mountains. There are several galleries I always like to visit when I'm there."

"Have a wonderful time, Bev."

Bev searched her face. "You'll be staying on here with Rafe?"

"Do you mind?"

Bev smiled. "Not at all. I'm delighted. I was afraid you might head straight back to Seattle. In fact I told Connor that perhaps we should cancel our plans in order to encourage you to stay here with us a little longer."

"I told her, forget it," Connor said as he walked past with a suitcase under each arm. He was followed by Tom who was carrying two more bags. "I was willing to help Cassidy get you down here but he's on his own now. I refuse to help him with any more of his courting work. I'm too busy tending to my own woman."

Bev's eyes lifted briefly toward the heavens. "Listen to the man."

Connor chuckled hugely as he put the suitcases into the trunk. He looked over at Rafe who was coming through the door with one last bag. "Hey, Cassidy. Tell your mother you can handle my daughter on your own from here on in. She's afraid Maggie's going to take off the minute our backs are turned."

Rafe's eyes met Margaret's. "Maggie's not going anywhere, are you, Maggie?"

Under the combined scrutiny of Bev, Tom, her father and her lover, Margaret felt herself turning pink. "Well, I had thought I might stay a few more days but that decision is subject to change if the pressure gets to be too much," she informed them all in dry tones.

"Pressure?" Rafe assumed an innocent, injured air. "What pressure? There's no pressure being applied, Maggie, love. Just bear in mind that if you take off this time, I'll be no more than fifteen minutes behind you and I won't be real happy."

"In that case, I suppose I might as well stay. As it happens, I have a social engagement here on Monday evening."

That succeeded in getting everyone's attention.

"What social engagement?" Rafe demanded. "You don't know anyone here in Tucson except me."

"That's not quite true, Rafe. I also know your sister and her friend Sean Winters. I've been invited to a showing of Sean's work."

"You're going to some damned art show?"

Margaret smiled serenely. "I thought you might like to escort me."

Rafe's brows came together in one solid, unyielding line. He slammed the trunk shut. "Like hell. We'll discuss this later."

Connor Lark turned to his fiancée. "Something tells me the children won't be bored while we're gone, dear. I think they're going to be able to entertain themselves just fine without us."

Bev glanced curiously from Margaret's cool, deliberate smile to Rafe's thunderous scowl. "Something tells me you're right, Connor."

Rafe stood beside Margaret as Connor drove away from the house. When the car was out of sight he took Margaret's arm and turned her firmly back into the foyer.

"Now tell me what the hell this business is about attending an exhibition of Winters's work."

"It's very simple. Julie and Sean invited me last night before they left. I accepted." She took a deep breath. "On behalf of both of us."

Rafe propped one shoulder against the wall in the negligent, dangerous pose he did so well. He folded his arms across his chest. "Is that right?"

Margaret cleared her throat delicately. "Yes. Right."

"What the devil do you think you're doing, Maggie?"

"Manipulating you into giving your sister's choice of a husband a fair chance?" She tried a smile to lighten the atmosphere.

"Trying to manipulate me is right. At least you're honest about it. But you should know me well enough by now to know I don't like being manipulated, not even by you. And what the hell do you mean my sister's choice of a *husband*? She told you she's actually thinking of marrying that damned artist?"

"They told me their plans last night. I think they have every intention of following through, Rafe, with or without your approval. You'd better learn to accept the situation graciously or risk alienating your sister."

"Damnation." Rafe came away from the wall and plowed his fingers through his hair. "Marry him? I didn't know they were that serious. I thought Winters was just another boyfriend. Julie's always got one or two trailing around behind her."

Margaret eyed him with a feeling of sympathy. "You've been looking after her for so long you may not have noticed she's grown up, Rafe. Julie's an adult woman. She makes her own choices."

"Some choices. She hasn't even been able to choose a job she can stay with for six months at a time. The guy's an artist, Maggie. Why couldn't she have found herself a nice, respectable . . ." His voice trailed off abruptly and he slid a quick glance at Margaret.

"A nice, respectable businessman? Someone who wears three-piece suits and ties and travels two weeks out of every month? Someone who needs an attractive, self-sacrificing hostess of a wife to entertain his guests while he closes big deals?"

Rafe winced. "Is that what you thought I'd turn you into? The boss's wife?"

"It's one of the things I was afraid of, yes."

"You should have said something."

"I tried. You never listened."

"I'm listening now," Rafe said evenly. His gaze locked with hers. "Believe me?"

Margaret nodded slowly. "Yes," she said, "I think I do."

Rafe nodded once. "Okay, that's settled. But that doesn't mean I'm going to approve of Winters."

"Rafe, they don't need your approval. They're quite capable of getting married without it."

"You think so?" Rafe's mouth twisted. "What if Winters finds out Julie doesn't come equipped with an unlimited checking account and a handful of charge cards?"

"I don't think he's marrying her for her money."

"How do you know? You only met him once last night."

"I liked him. And even if he is marrying her for her money, there's still not much you can do about it. Your best bet is to stay on good terms with your sister regardless of whether her decision is right or wrong."

"I could always try buying Winters off," Rafe said thoughtfully.

"I don't think that would be a very smart thing to do, Rafe. Julie would hate you for it. Give Sean a chance first before you try anything drastic. Come to the gallery show with me."

"Why? What will that prove?"

"It will give you an opportunity to meet him on his turf, instead of yours. If you're going to have him in the family you should make an effort to learn something about his world."

"Stop talking as if the marriage is an accomplished fact."

"Rafe, you're being deliberately stubborn and bullheaded about this. Give the man a chance. You know you should."

"Yeah? Why should I?" he challenged.

"I thought giving the other guy a fair chance was one of those fundamental tenets of the Code of the West."

He scowled ferociously at her. "What the devil are you talking abut now? What's this nonsense about a code?"

She smiled again. "You know that basic creed you probably learned at your father's knee. The one he undoubtedly got from his father and so on. The one that's supposed to cover little things like vengeance, honor, justice and fair play among the male of the species."

Rafe swore again in disgust and paced the length of the foyer. He stopped at the far end, swung around and eyed her for a short, tense moment. "You want to play by the Code of the West? All right, I'll go along with that. We'll start with a little simple frontier justice. If you want to manipulate me into going to that damn gallery, you've got to pay the price."

Margaret watched him with sudden wariness. "What price?"

Rafe smiled dangerously. "In exchange for my agreement to go to the showing, you agree to let me announce our engagement. I want it official, Maggie. No more fooling around."

Margaret took a deep breath. "All right."

Rafe stared at her in open astonishment. "You agree?"

"You've got yourself a deal, cowboy."

Rafe gave a shout of triumph. "Well, it's about time, lady."

He took one long stride forward, scooped Margaret up in his arms and carried her down the hall to the nearest bedroom.

This time he took off his boots.

8

RAFE SADDLED his best chestnut stallion the next morning at dawn. Out of the corner of his eye he watched with satisfaction as Maggie adjusted her own saddle on the gray mare. He took a quiet pleasure in the competent manner in which she handled the tack and the horse. Connor had been right. His daughter knew her way around a barn.

Rafe wondered how he could have spent two whole months with Maggie last year and never learned that single, salient fact about her.

Then again, those two months had passed in a tangled web of sudden, consuming passion mixed with an explosive game of corporate brinksmanship that had involved millions. There had been very little time for getting to know the small, intimate details of his new lover's past. He had been far too anxious to spend what little free time he had with her in bed.

Money and love were a dangerous combination, Rafe had discovered. A pity he hadn't learned to separate the two before. But, then, in all fairness to himself, he'd never come across the two combined in such a lethal fashion until last year.

He knew what he was doing this time around. He could handle both.

"All set?" he asked as he finished checking the cinch on his saddle.

"I'm ready." Margaret picked up the reins and led her mare toward the barn door.

"We'll ride out over the east foothills. I want to show you some land I'm thinking of selling." Rafe walked the chestnut out into the early morning light and vaulted lightly into the saddle. He turned his head to enjoy the sight of Maggie's sexy jeans-clad bottom as she mounted her mare. The woman looked good on horseback. Almost as good as she looked in bed. Rafe nudged the stallion with his knee and the chestnut moved forward with brisk eagerness.

The day was going to be hot, Rafe thought. They all were this time of year. But at this hour the desert was an unbelievably beautiful place—still cool enough to allow a man to enjoy the wide open, primitive landscape. It was a landscape that had always appealed strongly to something deep within him. They had never talked about it, but he'd always sensed the land had affected his father and his grandfather in the same way.

They rode in companionable silence until they came to the point where a wide sweep of the ranch could be seen. Only a handful of cattle were visible. Here in the desert livestock needed vast stretches on which to graze. The cattle tended to scatter widely.

Rafe halted the chestnut and waited for Margaret to bring her mare alongside. She did so, surveying the rolling foothills spread out in front of her.

"How much of this is Cassidy land?" she asked.

"Just about all of what you can see," Rafe admitted. "It goes up into the mountains. My great-grandfather acquired most of it. My grandfather and father added to it. They all ran cattle on it and did some mining in the hills. The land's been good to the Cassidys."

"But now you're thinking of selling it?"

Rafe nodded. "Some of it. It would be the smart thing to do. The truth is, the cattle business isn't what it used to be and probably won't ever be again. The mines are all played out. If I had any sense I would have gotten rid of the stock five years ago and sold the acreage to a developer who wants to put in a golf course and a subdivision."

"Why didn't you?"

"I don't know," he admitted. "Lord knows I don't need several thousand acres of desert. I've made my money buying and selling businesses, not in running cattle. Compared to my other investments, running livestock is more of a hobby than anything else. But for some reason I haven't been able to bring myself to put the land on the market."

"Maybe that's because part of you doesn't really think it's yours to sell. You inherited it so maybe you think deep down that you're supposed to hold it in trust for the next generation of Cassidys."

Rafe was startled by that observation. She was right, he thought. Absolutely right. "Sounds kind of feudal, doesn't it?"

"A bit old-fashioned in some ways," Margaret agreed. "But I can see the pull of that kind of philosophy. When you look at land like this you tend to start thinking in more fundamental terms, don't you?"

"Yeah. When I was younger I used to ride out here and do a lot of that kind of thinking. Then I got away from it for a while. I got back in the habit this past year."

"Because of me?"

"Yeah."

Margaret looked down at the reins running through her fingers. "I did a lot of thinking, too. It nearly drove me crazy for a while."

"I know what you mean." Rafe was silent for a moment, satisfied that they had both suffered during the past year. "You know, I really should sell this chunk of desert. There are plenty of developers who would pay me a fortune for it."

"Do you need another fortune?"

Rafe shrugged. "No. Not really."

"Then don't sell. At least not now." Maggie smiled her glowing smile, the one that always made him want to grab her and kiss her breathless. "Who knows, maybe the next generation of Cassidys won't be as good at wheeling and dealing in the business world as this generation is. Your descendents might need the land far more than you need more money. No one can predict the future and land is the one certain long-term investment. Hold on to it and let the next batch of Cassidys sell it if they need to do so."

"You mean, tell myself I really am holding it in trust for the family?"

"Yes."

Rafe looked out over the vastness in front of him. Maggie's simple logic suddenly made great sense. It was a relief somehow to be able to tell himself that there was no overwhelming need to sell for business reasons. "I think that's exactly what I'll do. I wonder why I didn't think of it that way before now."

"You've been thinking in terms of good business, as usual. But there are other things just as important. A family's heritage is one of them. My father sold his land because he had no choice. He turned out to be a much better engineer and businessman than he was a rancher. But a part of him has always regretted giving up the land. You're not forced to make the choice, so why do it?"

Rafe reached across the short distance between them and wrapped his hand around the nape of her neck. He leaned forward and kissed her soundly. He had to release her abruptly as the chestnut tossed his head and pranced to one side. Quickly Rafe brought the stallion back under control and then he grinned at Maggie.

"Remind me to bounce the occasional business problem off you in the future, Maggie, love. I like the way you think."

"Praise from Caesar." Her laugh was soft and somehow indulgent. "You do realize this is the first and only time you've ever asked my opinion on a business matter?"

"I'll obviously have to do it more often." Rafe hesitated a few seconds, not sure how to say what he intended to say next. Hell, he wasn't even certain he wanted to say it at all. But for some irrational reason he needed to do it. "Maggie, about our bargain."

She glanced at him in surprise. "What bargain?"

He was annoyed that she had forgotten already. "Don't give me that blank look, woman. I'm talking about the bargain we made the other day. The one in which I agreed to go to Winters's gallery show in exchange for your agreement to let me announce our engagement. Or has that little matter slipped your mind?"

She blinked, taken aback by his vehemence. "Hardly. I guess I just hadn't thought of it as a bargain."

"Yeah, well, that's what it was, wasn't it?"

"I suppose so. In a way. What's bothering you about it, Rafe?"

He exhaled heavily, willing himself to shut his mouth while there was still time. But the words came of their own accord. "I don't want you agreeing to get engaged because we've made a deal, Maggie. I don't like having you feel you've got to do it to defend Julie from my bullheaded stubbornness."

"Oh, Rafe, I really didn't think of it quite like that."

"All the same, I thought I'd tell you that I'll go to that damned art show with no strings attached. I'll give Winters a fair chance. As for us, you don't have to make any promises to me until you're ready. I'm willing to give you all the time you need to make certain you want to marry me."

"You surprise me, Rafe."

"I can see that." He was still irritated. "You don't have to look so stunned. You think I can't be open-minded when I want to be?"

"Well—"

"You think I can't give a guy a fair chance?"

"Well—"

"You think the only way I work is by applying pressure whenever I see an opportunity to do so?"

"Well, to be perfectly honest, Rafe . . ."

He held up a hand. "Forget it. I don't think I need a truthful answer to that one. But I am doing my best to back off a little here, so let me do it, okay?"

"Okay." She smiled gently.

Saddle leather creaked as he studied her face in the morning light. "I want you to marry me. But I want you to come to me willingly, Maggie, love. Not because I've pushed you into it." Rafe drew a deep breath and got the rash words out before he could rethink them. "Take all the time you need to make your decision."

"So long as I come up with the right one?" Her eyes danced mischievously.

He grinned slowly, relaxing inside. "You've got it. So long as it's the right one." The sun was getting higher in the morning sky and the heat was setting in already. Rafe crammed the brim of his hat down low over his eyes and turned the chestnut back toward the ranch.

IT WAS OBVIOUS from the moment Margaret and Rafe entered the thronged gallery that the showing of Sean Winters's work was a resounding success. The large, prestigious showroom was filled with well-dressed people sipping champagne and commenting learnedly on contemporary art. Margaret saw Rafe's cool-eyed appraisal of the gathering and smiled.

"Not quite what you expected, hmm, cowboy?"

"All right, I'll admit the man apparently has a market. The place is packed. That must be his stuff on the walls. Let's take a look at it before Julie discovers we're here."

Sean Winters's work was clearly of the Southwestern school, full of the rich, sun-drenched tones of the desert. His paintings for the most part tended toward the abstract with an odd hint of surrealism. There was a curiously hard edge to them that made them stand out from the work of other artists dealing with similar subject matter. Margaret was instantly enthralled.

"These are wonderful," she exclaimed, a bit in awe in spite of herself. "Look at that canyon, Rafe. And that evening sky above it."

Rafe peered more closely at the painting she indicated. "Are you sure it's a canyon? Looks like lots of little wavy lines of paint to me."

"It's titled *Canyon*, you twit. And don't you dare play the uncultured, uncouth redneck cowboy with me, Rafe. This work is good and you know it. Admit it."

"It's interesting. I'll give it that much." Rafe frowned at the price on the tag stuck next to the painting. "Also expensive. If Winters can really sell this stuff for this kind of money, he's got quite a racket going."

"Almost as good a racket as buying and selling companies."

Rafe gave her a threatening scowl just as Julie came hurrying up to greet them.

"You made it. I'm so glad. I was hoping you'd get him here, Margaret." Julie turned hopeful eyes on her brother. "Thanks for coming, Rafe. I really appreciate it."

"Thank Margaret. She practically hog-tied me and dragged me here. You know I'm not into the artsy-craftsy stuff."

Julie's sudden glowering expression bore a startling resemblance to the one Rafe could produce so quickly. "I'm not going to let you dismiss Sean's work as artsy-craftsy stuff, Rafe. Do you hear me? He is a very talented artist and the least you can do is show some respect."

"Okay, okay, calm down. I'm here, aren't I? I'm willing to give the guy a chance."

Julie glanced uncertainly from her brother to Margaret and back again. "You are?"

"Sure. Code of the West and all that."

"What are you talking about, Rafe?"

Rafe flashed a quick grin at Margaret, who beetled her brows at him. "Never mind."

Julie relaxed and gestured at the art that surrounded them. "Tell me the truth, Rafe. Now that you've had a chance to see it, what do you really think of Sean's work? Isn't it wonderful?"

Margaret didn't trust the response she saw forming in Rafe's eyes. She stepped in quickly to answer Julie's query. "Rafe was just saying how impressed he was, weren't you, Rafe?"

Rafe started to comment on that, caught Margaret's eye again and apparently changed his mind. "Uh, yeah. That's just what I was saying." He looked around as if seeking further inspiration. "Big crowd here tonight."

"Oh, there always is for a new showing of Sean's work. He's had a steady market for some time but lately he's been getting a lot of attention in reviews and articles. His career is definitely taking off."

Rafe nodded. "Things blow hot and cold in the art world, don't they? Not a reliable line of work. An artist can be in big demand one year and dead in the water the next."

Margaret saw Julie's mouth tighten and she turned to pounce on Rafe. But the attack proved unnecessary. Sean Winters had come up in time to hear the remark. He smiled coolly at Rafe.

"Nothing's for sure in the art world or any other. That's why I've paid a fair amount of attention to my investments since I made my first sale."

"Is that right?" Rafe swiped a glass of champagne from a passing tray and gave Sean a challenging look. "What do you put your money into, Winters, paint?"

"I guess you could say that. I own that artists' supply house Julie manages. We grossed a quarter of a million last year and this quarter's sales are already overtaking last quarter's. Or so I'm told. I just read the financial statements. I don't actively manage things. Julie handles everything."

Rafe nearly choked on his champagne. Margaret obligingly pounded him on the back. He gave her a sharp look.

"Sorry. Did I hit you too hard?" She smiled at him with brilliant innocence.

Rafe turned back to Winters. "Julie works for you? You own that place she's been managing for the past few months?"

"Best manager I've got."

"How many have you got?"

"Two. New store just opened in Phoenix last month. Julie's going to be overseeing the management of both branches. I don't like having to worry about the business side of things so I've turned it all over to your sister. She seems to have inherited her fair share of the family talent."

"I see," said Rafe. He took another swallow of champagne and glared around the room. "We've been looking at the paintings. Maggie likes your stuff."

Sean grinned. "Thanks, Margaret."

"It's stunning. I love it. If I could afford it, I'd buy *Canyon* in a red-hot second. Unfortunately it's a little out of my range."

Sean winced in chagrin. "I know. Ridiculous, isn't it? For a long time I couldn't even afford to buy my own stuff. I leave the pricing of my work up to Cecil."

"Who's Cecil?"

"He owns this gallery and one in Scottsdale and let me tell you, Cecil is one ruthless son of a gun." Sean grinned at Rafe. "Come to think of it, you'd probably like him, Cassidy. The two of you undoubtedly have a lot in common. Want to meet him?"

"Why not? I'd like to hear a little more about the inside workings of this art business." Rafe handed his empty glass to Margaret and strode off with Sean.

Margaret and Julie watched the two men make their way across the room for a moment and then Julie looked anxiously at Margaret. "Rafe's going to grill Sean. I just know it."

"I wouldn't worry. I have a feeling Sean can take care of himself."

Julie looked briefly surprised and then she relaxed slightly. "You're right. It's just that I've been defending and protecting my dates from Rafe for so long, it's become a habit. I get nervous whenever he gets near one. He tends to stampede them toward the nearest exit. And now that I've actually decided to marry Sean a part of me is terrified Rafe will scare him off."

"No chance of that," Margaret said cheerfully. "Sean won't scare easily." She turned back to study *Canyon*. "Why didn't you tell Rafe you were actually working for Sean?"

"I wanted to make sure I could make a success of the job before I told either Rafe or my mother. This is the first position I've gotten on my own, you know. Rafe has always taken it upon himself to line up something for me. He had a job waiting the day I graduated college. Said it was my graduation present. Every time I quit one he used his business contacts to line up another one."

"That's Rafe, all right. Tends to take over and run things if you let him."

Julie sighed. "The problem is he's good at running business things. You can't deny he's got a natural talent for it. But when he gets involved in people things he's dangerous."

Margaret laughed. "I know what you mean."

"How are you two doing up there at the ranch without Mom or Connor to referee?"

"We're slowly but surely reaching a negotiated peace."

Julie smiled. "I'm glad. Difficult as my brother is, I want him to be happy. And he definitely has not been happy this past year. Margaret, I want to thank you again for what you've done tonight. You didn't have to go out of your way to help. It was very kind of you."

"No problem. Rafe is basically a good man. He just needs a little applied management theory now and then. When it comes right down to it, he did it for you, Julie. You are his sister, after all."

"No," Julie said with a smile. "He didn't do it for me. He did it for you."

RAFE SHUDDERED HEAVILY and muffled his shout of sensual satisfaction against the pillow under Maggie's head. The echo of her own soft cries still hovered in the air along with the scent of their lovemaking. A moment earlier he had felt the tiny, delicate ripples of her release and he had been pulled beyond the limits of his self-control.

She always had this effect on him, Rafe thought as he relaxed slowly. She had the power to unleash this raging torrent of physical and emotional response within him. When their lovemaking was over he was always left with an incredible sense of well-being. There was nothing else on earth quite like it.

Rafe rolled off Maggie's slick, nude body and settled on his back, one hand under his head. He left his other hand lying possessively on one of Maggie's sweetly rounded thighs.

For a long while they were silent together, just as they always were when they rode into the hills at dawn. In some ways making love with Maggie was a lot like taking her riding, Rafe told himself. He grinned suddenly into the moonlit shadows.

"What's so funny?" Maggie stretched luxuriously and turned onto her side. She put her hand on his chest.

"Nothing. I was just thinking that being with you like this is a little like riding with you."

"I don't want to hear any crude cracks about midnight rodeos."

"All right, ma'am. No crude cracks." He smiled again. "Midnight rodeo? Where'd you get a phrase like that? You've been sneaking around listening to country-western music stations, haven't you?"

"I refuse to answer that." She snuggled closer. "But for the record, I will tell you that you're terrific in the saddle."

"I was born to ride," Rafe said with patently false modesty. "And you're the only little filly I ever want to get on top of."

"Uh-huh. Keep it that way. Tell me what you talked about with Sean Winters tonight at the gallery."

"It was men's talk," Rafe said loftily and was promptly punished by having his chest hair yanked quite severely. "Sheesh, okay, okay, lay off the torture. I'll talk."

"Yes?"

"We discussed business."

"Business?"

"Yeah. The business of the art world. It's real dog-eat-dog, did you know that? Bad as the corporate world. We also talked about the fact that he fully intends to marry Julie. With or without my approval."

"And?"

Rafe shifted slightly on the pillow. "And what?"

"And did you try to buy him off?"

"That's none of your business."

"You did, didn't you?" Maggie sat up abruptly, glaring down at him. "Rafe, I warned you not to try that."

He studied her breasts in the moonlight. She had beautiful breasts he told himself, trying to be objective about it. They fit perfectly into his palms. "Don't worry, we got the issue settled."

"What issue?"

"Winters's paintings are for sale, but he isn't," Rafe explained succinctly.

Maggie flopped back down onto the pillow. "I told you so."

"Yeah, you did, didn't you? Has anyone ever told you that's a nasty habit?" Rafe asked conversationally.

"Saying 'I told you so'?" She turned her head and gave him a sassy grin. "But I'm good at it."

He gave her an affectionate slap on her sleek hip and yawned. "You're good at it, all right. I'll have to admit it looks like the Cassidys are going to have an artist in their ranks."

"You're beginning to like Sean, aren't you?"

"He's okay."

"And you're going to tell Julie you like him and approve of him, aren't you?"

"Probably," Rafe admitted. He was feeling too complacent and sensually replete to argue about anything right now.

Maggie giggled delightfully in the darkness. "I love you when you're like this."

"Like what?"

"So reasonable."

Rafe felt a cold chill go through him. The satisfaction he had been feeling a few seconds ago vanished. He thought of the file in his study and the moves he had instructed Hatcher to make that morning. He levered himself up onto one elbow and looked down at the woman beside him.

She sensed the change in him instantly. "Rafe? What's wrong?"

"What about when I'm not reasonable by your standards, Maggie?" he asked. "Will you still love me?"

She searched his face, her eyes soft and shadowed. "Yes."

Rafe inhaled deeply and told himself she meant it. "Say it straight out for me. I need to hear the words."

"I love you, Rafe." She touched his shoulder, her fingers gliding down his arm in a gentle caress. "I never stopped loving you although I will admit I tried very hard."

Rafe fell back onto the pillow and pulled her down across his chest. He drove his fingers through her tangled hair and held her head clasped in his hands. "I love you, Maggie. I want you to always remember that."

"I will, Rafe."

He lay there looking up at her for a while and then the tension went out of him. His good mood restored itself. "Does this mean we're finally engaged?"

She smiled slowly. "Why, yes, I guess it does."

"You're sure?" he pressed. "You're willing to set a date?"

Maggie nodded. "Yes. If you're very sure you want to marry me."

"I've never been more certain of anything in my life." He used the grip in her hair to pull her mouth closer to his own. When he kissed her, she parted her lips for him, letting him deep inside where he could stake his intimate claim. Rafe growled softly as he felt himself start to grow hard again.

Maggie giggled.

"What are you laughing at, lady?"

"You sound like a big cat when you do that."

He rolled to the edge of the bed, taking her with him. Then he stood up with her in his arms. Maggie laughed up at him as she clung to his neck. "What are you doing? Where are we going?"

"Swimming."

"But it's two in the morning."

"We can sleep late."

"We're both stark naked."

He grinned and eyed her body appreciatively. "That's true."

"You're impossible, you know that?"

"But you love me anyway, right?"

"Right." Maggie looked down as he reached the pool. She glanced up again in alarm as she realized his intentions. "I don't mind a late night swim, but don't you dare drop me into that water, Rafe."

"It's not cold."

She gave him a quelling look. "All the same, I do not like entering swimming pools by being dropped into them."

"Think of this as just another little example of simple frontier justice."

"Rafe, don't you dare. What justice are you talking about, anyway?"

"This is for trying to set me up at that gallery this evening."

Her eyes widened innocently. "But you agreed to go to the show with no strings attached. You said you liked Sean after you got to know him."

Rafe shook his head deliberately. "That's not the point. The point is you tried to set me up. Tried to manipulate me into doing exactly what you wanted. If you're going to play games like that, Maggie, love, you have to be prepared to pay the price." He opened his arms and let her fall.

She yelled very nicely as she went into the water. When she surfaced she promptly splashed him, laughing exuberantly as he tried to dodge.

Rafe grinned back at her and then dove into the pool thinking that this was probably one of the best nights of his entire life.

9

RAFE WAITED until Margaret's back was turned in the large mall bookstore before he strolled casually over to the romance section. He stood there for a moment, lost in a sea of lushly illustrated paperbacks. Then he spotted a familiar-looking name. Fuchsia foil spelled out Margaret Lark. The title of the book was *Ruthless*.

After another quick glance to make certain that Margaret was still busy browsing through mysteries, Rafe examined the cover of her latest book. It showed a man and a woman locked in a passionate embrace. The man had removed the charcoal gray jacket of his suit and his tie hung rakishly around his neck. His formal white shirt was open to the waist and his hand was behind the lady's back, deftly lowering the zipper of her elegant designer gown.

The couple was obviously standing in the living room of a sophisticated penthouse. In the backdrop high-rise buildings rose into a dark sky and the sparkling lights of a big city glittered.

Rafe opened *Ruthless* to the first page and started to read.

"It's no secret, Anne. The man's a shark. Just ask anyone who worked for any of the companies Roarke Cody is supposed to have salvaged in the past five years. He may have saved the firms but he did it by firing most of the management and supervisory level people. We're all going to be on the street in a week, you mark my words."

Anne Jamison picked up the stack of files on her desk and glanced at her worried assistant. "Calm down, Brad. Cody's been hired to straighten out this company, not decimate the staff. He must be good to have acquired the reputation he's got. Now, if you'll excuse me, I've got to get going. I've got a meeting in his office in five minutes."

"Anne, you're not listening. The guy's ruthless. Don't you understand?" Brad trailed after her to the door. "He's probably called you into his office to fire you. And after he lets you go, I'm next. You'll see."

Anne pretended to ignore her frantic assistant as she made her way down the hall, but the truth was, she was not nearly as confident as she looked. She was as aware of Cody's reputation as Brad was—more so, in fact, because she'd done some checking.

"Ruthless" was, indeed, the right word to describe the turnaround specialist who had been installed here at the corporate headquarters of Seaco Industries. Roarke Cody had left a trail of fired personnel in his wake wherever he had gone to work. He was nothing less than a professional hit man whose gun was for hire by any company that could afford him.

Three minutes later Anne was shown into the new gunslinger's office. She held her breath as the tall, lean, dark-haired man standing at the window turned slowly to face her. One look and her heart sank. She had been putting up a brave, professional front but the fact was, she had known the full truth about this man the first day she'd met him. There was no mercy in those tawny gold eyes—no compassion in that hard, grim face.

"Good morning, Mr. Cody," she said with the sort of gallant good cheer one adopted in front of a firing squad. "I understand you're on the hunt and you'll be having most of management for dinner."

"Not most of management." Roarke's deep voice was tinged with a hint of a Western drawl. "Just you, Miss Jamison. Seven o'clock tonight." He smiled without any humor. "I thought we might discuss your immediate future."

Anne's mouth fell open in shock. "Mr. Cody, I couldn't possibly..."

"Perhaps I should clarify that. It's not just your future we will discuss," he said smoothly. "But that of your staff, as well."

And suddenly Anne knew exactly how it felt to be singled out as prey.

"For heaven's sake, what are you doing?" Margaret hissed in Rafe's ear.

"Reading one of your books." Rafe closed *Ruthless* and smiled blandly. "Something sort of familiar about this Roarke guy."

To his surprise, Margaret blushed a vivid pink. "You're imagining things. Put that back and let's go get that coffee you promised me."

"Hang on a second, I want to buy this." Rafe reached for his wallet as he started toward the counter.

Margaret hurried after him. "You're going to buy *Ruthless*? But, Rafe, it's not exactly your kind of book."

"I'm not so sure about that."

She stifled a groan and retreated to wait near the door as Rafe paid for the book. A moment later, his package in one hand, Rafe ambled out into the air-conditioned mall. "Okay, let's get the coffee."

Margaret marched determinedly toward a small café near a fountain and sat down. "Are you really going to read that?"

"Uh-huh. Why don't you have your coffee and go shop for a while? I'll just sit here and read."

"Why this sudden interest in my writing?"

"Maggie, love, I want to know everything there is to know about you. Besides, I'm curious to see whether or not I save Seaco Industries."

"Whether or not *you* save it," she gasped in outrage. "Rafe, don't get any ideas about my having used you as a model for the hero in my book."

Rafe paid no attention to that as he dug *Ruthless* out of the sack and put it down on the table in front of him. "Come on, Maggie, love. Light brown eyes, dark brown hair and a Western drawl? Who do you think you're kidding?"

"I have news for you, Rafe. There are millions of men around who fit that description."

"Yeah, but I'm the one you know," he said complacently as he ordered two cups of coffee from a hovering waitress.

Margaret gave him an exasperated glare. "You want to know something? Most of my heroes look like Roarke Cody. And I wrote at least three of them long before I ever met you."

"Is that right? No wonder you fell straight into my hands the day I met you. I was your favorite hero come to life. The man of your dreams."

"Why you arrogant cowboy. Of all the . . ."

"Give me a hint," Rafe said, interrupting her casually. "Does the heroine sleep with this Roarke guy in the hope that she can persuade him not to fire her and her staff?"

"Of course not." Margaret was obviously scandalized at the suggestion. "That would be highly unethical. None of my heroines would do such a thing."

"Hmm. But he tries to get her to do that, right?"

Margaret lifted her chin. "Roarke Cody is quite ruthless in the beginning. He tries all sorts of underhanded, sneaky maneuvers to get the heroine."

"And?"

"And what?"

"Do any of those underhanded, sneaky maneuvers work as well as the underhanded, sneaky maneuver I used to get you down here to Tucson?"

Margaret folded her arms on the table and leaned forward with a belligerent glare. "I am not going to tell you the plot."

"Go shopping, Maggie, love. I'll wait right here for you." Rafe propped one booted heel on a convenient empty chair, leaned back and picked up *Ruthless*.

MARGARET SPENT OVER AN HOUR in the colorful, Southwestern-style shops. The air-conditioned shopping mall was crowded with people seeking to escape the midday heat.

The clothes featured in the windows tended to be brighter and more casual in style than what she was accustomed to seeing in Seattle. It made for an interesting shopping experience that she deliberately lengthened in the hope of causing Rafe to grow bored and restless.

But when she returned to the indoor sidewalk café, several packages in hand, she saw to her dismay that he was still deep into *Ruthless*.

She told herself she ought to find his interest in her book gratifying or at the very least somewhat amusing. But the fact was, it made her uncomfortable. He had guessed the truth immediately. He was the hero of *Ruthless* and of every book she had ever written.

Margaret had been in the middle of writing Roarke and Anne's story when she had met Rafe. She had finished it shortly after Rafe had turned on her and accused her of betraying him. It had not been easy to write a happy ending when her own lovelife was in shambles.

But a part of her had sought to work out in *Ruthless* the ending that had been denied to her in real life. Her own relationship might have gone on the rocks but she'd still had her dreams of what a good relationship could be. A woman had to have faith in the future.

"Not finished yet?" Margaret came to a halt in front of Rafe.

He looked up slowly. "Gettin' there. Ready to go?"

She nodded. "I could use a swim."

"Good idea." Rafe got to his feet and dropped *Ruthless* back into the paper bag. "You know this Roarke guy started out okay in the beginning. He had the right idea about how to save Seaco. You've got to cut a lot of dead wood when you go into a situation like that. But I get the feeling he's being set up for a fall."

"He's being set up for a happy ending," Margaret muttered.

Rafe shook his head, looking surprisingly serious. "The problem is, he's starting to let his hormones make his decisions. He's getting soft." Rafe chuckled. "Not in bed, I'll grant you, he's holding up just fine there. But when it comes to business, he's falling apart. Going to shoot himself in the foot if he doesn't get back on track."

"He's falling in love with the heroine and that love is causing him to change," Margaret snapped.

"It's causing him to act stupid."

"Rafe, for pity's sake, it's just a story. Don't take it so seriously."

"Real life business doesn't work like that."

"It's a story, Rafe. A romance."

"You know," Rafe said, looking thoughtful as they walked out of the mall into the furnace of the parking lot, "your dad was right. It's a good thing you got out of the business world, Maggie. You're not tough enough for it."

"My father said that? I'll strangle him."

"He said it during one of our early conversations and I agree."

"You're both a couple of turkeys."

"Maybe women in general just aren't hard enough to make it in the business world," Rafe continued philosophically. "You've got to be willing to be ruthless, really ruthless or you'll get eaten by the bigger sharks. Women, especially women like you, just don't have that extra sharp edge, know what I mean?"

Margaret came to a full halt right in the middle of the blazing parking lot and planted herself squarely in front of a startled Rafe. She was hotter than the blacktop on which she stood, her anger suddenly lashed into a fire storm.

"Why you chauvinistic, pig-headed, redneck cowboy. I always had a feeling that deep down inside you didn't approve of women in the business world and now at last the truth comes out. So you don't think women can handle it, do you? You don't think we'll ever make it in big business? That we aren't ruthless enough?"

"Now, honey, it was just an observation."

"It's a biased, prejudiced, masculine observation. I've got news for you, Rafe Cassidy, one of these days women are going to not only make it big in the business world, but we're going to change the way it operates."

Rafe blinked and reached up to pull the brim of his Stetson lower over his eyes. "Is that right?"

"Darn right. You men have been running it long enough and women are getting tired of playing by your rules. We're getting tired of cutthroat business practices and vicious competition—tired of playing the game for the sake of some man's ego."

Rafe shrugged. "That's the way it works, Maggie, love. It's a jungle out there."

"Only because men have made it into one. I suppose that after you got civilized and no longer had the thrill of the hunt for real, you had to create a new way to get your kicks. So you turned all your aggressive instincts into the way you do business. But that's going to change as women take over."

"Uh, Maggie, love, it's kind of hot out here. What do you say we go back to the ranch and continue this fascinating discussion in the swimming pool?"

"Your sister is a good example of the new breed of female businessperson. And Sean Winters has shown the good sense to turn his stores over to her to manage. You could take a lesson from him."

A small smile edged Rafe's mouth. His eyes gleamed in the shadow of his hat. "You want me to turn Cassidy and Company over to you?"

"Of course not. I don't want anything to do with that company. I've got my own career in writing and I like it. But I swear to God, Rafe, if we have a daughter and if she shows an interest in the family business, you'd darn well better let her have a hand in it."

Rafe grinned slowly. "It's a deal. Let's go home and work on it."

Margaret stared at him in frowning confusion as he took her arm and steered her toward the Mercedes. "What are you talking about?"

"Our daughter. Let's go home and get busy making one. I want to see this brave new world of business once the women take over. The sooner we get started producing the new female executive, the sooner we'll see if it's going to work."

Margaret felt as if the wind had been knocked out of her. She struggled for air. "A daughter? Rafe, are you talking about a baby?"

"Yeah. Any objections?"

She cleared her throat, still dazed by the abrupt change of topic. A baby—Rafe's baby. A little girl to inherit his empire. Margaret recovered from her initial shock and began to smile gloriously.

"Why, no, Rafe. I don't have any objections at all."

RAFE WAS FEELING exceptionally good two days later when he walked down the hall to his study. He had no premonition of disaster at all.

But, then, he'd been feeling very good every day since Margaret had arrived. Now that they had the house to themselves he was indulging himself in the luxury of waking up beside her in the mornings. He loved that time at dawn when they lay together in tangled white sheets and watched the morning light pour over the mountains.

One of these days he really was going to have to start going back into the office on a regular basis, he told himself. But all in all, if the truth be known, he was slightly amazed at how well things were going with him on vacation.

He chuckled to himself at the thought that he might not be as indispensable at Cassidy and Company headquarters as he'd always assumed. Maggie wouldn't hesitate to point that out to him if he gave her the chance.

He rounded the corner, glancing at his watch. Hatcher had gone back out to his car to get another file. They had been working for the past two hours before taking a break and now they were going to finish the business. Rafe was looking forward to joining Margaret out by the pool.

Rafe walked through the door of his study, frowning slightly as he realized he must have left it open. Perhaps Hatcher had already returned from the car.

But it wasn't Doug Hatcher standing beside the desk staring at the open file and the computer printout lying alongside. It was Margaret. One look at her face and Rafe knew she had seen too much.

He sighed inwardly. He would much rather she hadn't found out what was going on, but it wasn't the end of the world, either. She loved him and this time around she was firmly in his camp.

"What are you doing in here, Maggie? I thought you were going swimming."

She was staring at him with wide eyes. A storm was brewing rapidly in their aqua depths. "Doug said you were in here. I wanted to talk to you. But I found this instead." She gestured angrily at the open file. "What in the world is going on, Rafe? What are you up to with this Ellington takeover? Why all these references to Moorcroft?"

"It's just business, Maggie, love. I'll be finished in another half hour or so. You told me you were willing to be reasonable about the amount of time I spent on work. Why don't you go on out to the pool?"

"This is what you were working on that night I found you in here after the engagement party, isn't it? This is why Hatcher comes here to see you every day. I demand to know what is going on."

"Why?"

"Why? Because it's clear Moorcroft is involved in some way and I know you have no liking for him." Her eyes narrowed. "I also know that you're quite capable of plotting revenge. Tell me the truth, Rafe. Are you in competition with Jack to take over Ellington?"

He shrugged and sat down behind the desk. "You could say that."

"What do you mean by that? Are you or aren't you?"

Rafe closed the damning file and regarded her consideringly. She was getting mad but she wasn't going up in flames. "As I said, Maggie, this is just business. It doesn't concern you."

"Are you sure? If this really is just business as usual, you're right. It doesn't concern me. But if this is some sort of vengeance against Jack, I won't have it."

Rafe rested his elbows on the arms of his chair and steepled his fingers. His initial uneasiness was over and he was starting to get annoyed by her attitude. "You think you have to protect Moorcroft? The way you did last year?"

She flinched at that. "No, of course not. I don't work for him any longer and I don't owe him anything, but—"

"You're right. You don't owe him anything, especially not your loyalty. That should be crystal clear this time around. So let him take his chances out there in the jungle, Maggie. He's been doing it a long time, same as me."

"Rafe, I don't like this. If you're up to something, I think I should be told."

"You're a romance writer these days, not a business executive. You don't need to know anything about this."

"Damn you, Rafe, don't you dare patronize me. I don't trust you to treat Moorcroft the way you would any other business competitor. Not after what happened last year. I want to know—" She broke off abruptly, glancing at the open door.

Rafe followed her gaze and saw Hatcher standing on the threshold. He looked uncertain of what he should do next. "I'll, uh, come back later, Rafe."

"No," Rafe said. "Maggie was just leaving. Come on in, Hatcher. I want to get this Ellington thing finished today. Sit down."

Margaret hesitated a moment and then apparently thought better of making a scene in front of Hatcher. "We'll discuss this later, Rafe." She turned and stalked out the door, the elegant line of her spine rigidly straight with anger.

Hatcher stared after her, looking more uneasy than ever. "She knows about the Ellington deal?"

"She walked in here and saw the damned file lying on the desk."

Hatcher paled. "Sorry. I know you didn't want her to find out about it."

Rafe bit off a curse. "It wasn't your fault. Never mind, I'll deal with Maggie later. I can sugarcoat the facts and calm her down. Let's get back to work."

Hatcher drew a deep breath. "Rafe, I think there's something you should know."

"What?" Rafe jabbed at a key on the computer console and narrowed his eyes as a familiar spreadsheet popped onto the screen.

"There's been another leak of information."

That caught Rafe's attention. He swung his gaze back to his assistant. "Bad?"

"The latest set of offer figures. The ones we drew up this week. My inside information tells me Moorcroft has them."

"This time around we were very, very careful, Hatcher," Rafe said softly. "Only you and I knew those numbers and they existed only in this file. We wiped them out of the computer after we ran the calculations."

Hatcher studied the desktop for a long moment before he looked up. There was a desperate expression in his eyes. "You're going to have my head if I say what I have to say next, Rafe."

Rafe looked at the man he had trusted for the past three years. "Just say it and get it over with."

"There's been someone else here in your house with access to these figures for over a week. I hate to be the one to point this out to you, but the fact is the really bad leaks began after she got here."

Rafe was so stunned he couldn't even think for a moment. The accusation against Margaret was the last thing he'd been expecting to hear. He had prepared himself for something else entirely.

For an instant he simply stared at Hatcher and then he came up out of the chair, grabbed his startled assistant by the collar of his immaculate shirt and yanked him halfway across the desk. "What the hell are you trying to tell me?"

Fear flashed in Hatcher's eyes. "Rafe, I'm sorry. I shouldn't have said anything. But someone has to point it out to you. And as long as it's gone this far, there's more you should know."

"More?" Rafe's hand tightened.

Hatcher looked down at the corded muscles of Rafe's forearms and then up again. "My sources tell me she saw him shortly before leaving Seattle to come down here."

"Hatcher, I swear, I'll break your neck if you're lying to me."

"It's true," Hatcher gasped. "I've known about the meeting for a couple of days but I've been afraid to tell you. But now you're practically accusing me of being the leak and I've got my own reputation to consider. Ask her. Go on, ask her if she didn't talk to Moorcroft before she flew to Tucson."

"There's no way she would have talked to that bastard."

"Is that right? Ask her if Jack Moorcroft didn't offer her a nice chunk of change to find out what she could about what we're up to. You want to pinpoint the leak? Don't look at me. I've been your man since the day I came to work for you. I've proven my loyalty a hundred times over. Try looking close to home, Rafe."

"Damn it, Hatcher, you don't know what you're saying."

"Yes, I do. I've just been afraid to say it out loud for several days because I knew you didn't want to hear it.

But you've never paid me to be a yes man, Rafe. You've always said you wanted me to speak my mind and tell you the facts as I saw them. All right, I'm doing just that. She betrayed you once and she's betraying you again."

Rafe felt himself hovering on the brink of his self-control. He hadn't been this close to going over the edge since the day he'd found Margaret with Moorcroft.

He made himself release his grip on Hatcher. Doug inhaled deeply and stepped quickly back out of reach, smoothing his clothing.

"Get out of here, Hatcher."

Hatcher glanced nervously at the file. "What about the Ellington deal? We need another set of numbers and we need them fast. We've got to make the final move within the next forty-eight hours."

"I said, get out of here."

Hatcher nodded quickly, picked up his briefcase and went to the door. There he paused briefly, his expression anguished. "Rafe, I'm sorry it turned out this way."

"Just go, will you?"

Hatcher nodded and went out the door without a backward glance.

Rafe stared for a long while at the far wall before he yanked open the bottom desk drawer and pulled out a glass and a bottle of Scotch.

Very carefully he poured the liquor into the glass and then he propped his feet on the desktop and leaned back in the chair. He took a long swallow of the potent Scotch and forced his mind to go blank for a full minute.

When he felt the icy calm close in on him he knew he had himself back under control.

"Rafe?"

He didn't turn his head. "Come in, Maggie."

"I heard Doug leave." She walked into the room and sat down on the other side of the desk. Her beautiful, clear eyes met his. "I want to have that discussion now, Rafe. I want to know what's going on and what you're planning to do to Moorcroft. Because if you're bent on getting vengeance on him for what happened last year—"

"Maggie."

Her brows drew together sharply as he interrupted her. "What?"

"Maggie, I have a couple of simple questions to ask you and I don't want any long, involved lectures or explanations. Just a simple yes or no."

"Rafe, are you all right? Is something wrong?"

"Something is wrong, but we'll get to that later. Just answer the questions."

"Very well, what are the questions?"

"Did you have a meeting with Jack Moorcroft in Seattle before you caught the plane to Tucson? Did he ask you to spy on me?"

The shock in her lovely eyes was all the answer he needed. Rafe swore softly and took another long pull on the Scotch.

"How did you know about that?" Margaret whispered in disbelief.

"Does it matter?"

"Yes, it bloody well matters," she shouted, slamming her fist on the desk. "I'd like to know what's going on around here and who's spying on me. I'd also like to know exactly what I stand accused of."

"Someone's been leaking information on the Ellington deal to Moorcroft. You, me and Doug Hatcher are the only ones who've had access to the file in the past few days. Just how badly did you hate my guts after what happened last year, Maggie, love? Bad enough to come back so that you could get a little revenge?"

"How dare you?" Margaret was on her feet. "*How dare you?*"

"Sit down, Maggie."

"I will not sit down, you deceitful, distrusting, son of a . . ." She gulped air. "I will not go through this a second time. Do you hear me? I won't let you tear me apart into little pieces again the way you did last time. You don't have to throw me out, Rafe. Not this time. I'm already gone."

She whirled and ran from the room.

Rafe finished the last swallow of Scotch and threw the glass against the wall. It shattered into a hundred glittering pieces and cascaded to the floor.

10

RAGE, A FIERCE, BURNING RAGE that was an agony to endure drove Margaret from the study. Behind her she thought she heard the crash of breaking glass but she paid no attention. She fled down the hall to her bedroom, dashed inside and slammed the door.

She was gasping for breath, the hot tears burning behind her eyes as she sank down onto the bed. An instant later she leaped up again, hugging herself in despair as she paced the room.

How could he do this to her a second time? she asked herself wildly. How could he doubt her now?

She had to get out of here. She could not bear to stay here under Rafe's roof another minute. Margaret ran to the mirrored chest and threw open the doors. She found her suitcase, dragged it out and tossed it onto the bed. Spinning around, she grabbed her clothes and began throwing them into the open suitcase.

He didn't trust her. That was what it came down to. After all they'd each been through separated this past year and after finally rediscovering their love for each other, Rafe still didn't trust her. He was prepared to believe she'd come here as a spy.

Damn Moorcroft, anyway. If only he hadn't looked her up that day in Seattle. If only she hadn't agreed to have coffee with him.

But if it hadn't been that unfortunate incident, it probably would have been something else sooner or later. Rafe was obviously ready to believe the worst.

And apparently he had a reason to worry about a Moorcroft spy, Margaret thought vengefully. He was plotting some form of revenge against his old rival. She just knew it. She was caught in the middle again between the two men and she was furious. They had no right to do this to her.

She would take the Mercedes, Margaret told herself. The keys were on the hall table. Rafe could damn well make arrangements to get his car out of the airport lot.

It was intolerable that he had dared to question her reason for being here in Tucson. He was the one who had forced her to come down here in the first place.

Margaret tossed one sandal into the suitcase and looked around for the other. She dropped to her knees to peer under the bed and to her horror, the tears started to fall.

It was too much.

She cried there on the floor until the rage finally burned itself out. Then, wearily, she climbed to her feet and went into the bathroom to wash her face.

She grimaced at the sight of herself in the mirror and reached for a brush. She wondered if Rafe was still in the study.

It flashed through her mind that he probably wouldn't come after her a second time. No, not a chance. In his own way he had sacrificed his pride once before to get her back and that was all anyone could reasonably expect. He was, when all was said and done, a tough, arrogant cowboy who was as hard and unforgiving as the desert itself.

And she loved him.

Heaven help her, she loved him. Margaret stared at herself in the mirror knowing that if she walked out this time, he would not come after her.

There was only one chance to salvage the situation. She was woman enough to know that this time she would have to be the one who rose above her own pride.

She forced herself to think back on the past few days. She clung to the knowledge that Rafe had changed since last year. He had tried hard to modify his work habits and to realign some of his priorities. He had worked hard to please her, to make her fall in love with him.

In his own way, he had tried to prove that he loved her.

Slowly Margaret put the brush back down on the counter. Turning on her heel, she went back through the bedroom and into the hall. The first few steps took all the willpower she had. Her instinct was to turn and run again but she kept going.

She rounded the corner and saw Rafe leaning in the open doorway of the study, thumb hooked onto his belt. In his other hand he coolly tossed the keys to the Mercedes. He watched her with an unreadable expression. Margaret halted. For a moment they just stared at each other and then Rafe broke the charged silence.

"Looking for these?" he asked, giving the keys another toss.

"No," Margaret said, starting forward deliberately. "No, I do not want the keys to the Mercedes."

"How are you going to get to the airport? You expect me to drive you?"

"That won't be necessary. I am not going to the airport."

"Sure you are. You're going to run, just like you did last time."

"Damn you, Rafe, I did not run away from you last year, I was *kicked out*."

"Depends on your point of view, I guess."

"It is not a point of view, it's a fact." Margaret came to a halt right in front of him and lifted both hands to grab him by the open collar of his shirt. She stood on tiptoe and brought her face very close to his. "Listen up, cowboy. I have a few more facts to tell you. And you, by heaven, are going to pay attention this time."

"Yeah?"

"Yeah." She pushed him backward into the study, too incensed and too determined to pursue her mission to notice just how easily he went. She forced him all the way back to his chair and then she put her hands on his shoulders and pushed downward. Rafe sat.

Margaret released him and stalked around to the other side of the desk. She planted her hands on the polished wood surface and leaned forward.

"If this were a romance novel instead of the real world, this little scene would not be necessary. Because of our great love for each other, you would trust me implicitly, you see. You would know without being told that I would never go to bed with you and then turn around and spy on you so that I could report to Moorcroft."

"Is that right? Your heroes can read minds?"

"The bonds of love make them intuitive, sensitive and insightful and don't you dare mock me, Cassidy."

"I thought I made it clear I'm not one of those modern, sensitive types."

"All right, all right, I accept the fact that this is not a romance novel and you are not exactly the most perceptive, intuitive man I've ever met."

"I'm no romance hero, that's for sure."

She ignored that. "I also accept the fact that I cannot expect you to come after me if I leave here today. You gave us both a second chance, Rafe. It's my turn to give us a third. I only hope this does not indicate a pattern for the future. Now then, let's get one thing straight. I did not make any deal with Jack Moorcroft."

Rafe waited in stony silence.

This was going to be hard, Margaret thought. Resolutely she gathered her courage. "I had not seen or heard from Jack Moorcroft since that debacle last year until he showed up out of the clear blue sky on the Saturday before I was due to come down here."

"Just a friendly visit, right?"

"No, you know very well it was not a friendly visit. He said he thought you might be plotting against him. He told me that since last year he's had the impression you were gunning for him. He thinks you're out to get him."

"I never said Moorcroft was a stupid man. He's right."

"He also said that he would give a great deal to know exactly what you were planning."

"Why didn't you mention the little fact that you'd seen him before you came down here?"

"Are you kidding? The last thing I wanted to do was mention Moorcroft to you. Keeping quiet was an act of pure self-defense. The last time I got between the two of you I got crushed, if you will recall."

"Damn it, Maggie . . ."

"Besides, I told him to take a flying leap. I made it clear I considered myself out of it. I did not work for him any longer. I owed him nothing this time around. I told him I was going to Tucson for my own personal reasons and that was that."

"And he accepted your answer?"

"Rafe, I swear I haven't communicated with him since that Saturday and I certainly have not handed over any of your precious secrets to him. I don't even know any of your secrets."

"You saw the Ellington file."

"I saw it for the first time this afternoon." Margaret closed her eyes and then opened them to pin him with a desperate gaze. "Rafe, I can't prove any of this. I am begging you to believe me. If Moorcroft has numbers he shouldn't have, then you must believe he got them from someone else. Please, Rafe. I love you too much to betray you."

"Revenge is a powerful motivator, Maggie," Rafe finally said quietly.

"More powerful for you than for me, Rafe."

"Are you sure of that?"

"I love you. When you came back into my life you opened up a wound I had hoped was healed. I was angry at first and frightened. And I didn't know if I could trust you. But I knew for certain the first night I was here that I still loved you."

"Maggie . . ."

"Wait, let me finish. Julie said something about what it had cost you in pride to find a way to get me back.

She was right. I realize that now that I'm standing here trampling all over my own pride in an effort to get you to trust me enough to believe in me. Please, Rafe, don't ruin what we've got. It's too precious and too rare. Please trust me. I didn't betray you."

"You love me?"

"I love you."

"Okay, then it must have been Hatcher, after all."

Margaret blinked. "I beg your pardon?"

"I said it must have been Hatcher who gave Moorcroft the numbers. He's been acting weird for the past six months or so, but I wasn't sure he would have the guts to actually sell me out. Hatcher's not what you'd call a real gutsy guy. Still, you never can tell, so I put some garbled preliminary information into the Ellington file to see what would happen."

"Rafe, will you please be quiet for a moment. I am having trouble following this conversation."

His brows rose. "Why? You started it."

She eyed him cautiously, uncertain of his mood. For one horrible second she thought he was actually laughing at her. But that made no sense. "Are you saying you believe me?"

"Maggie, love, I'd probably believe you if you told me you could get me a great deal on snowballs in hell."

She was dumbfounded. Slowly she sank into the nearest chair. "I don't understand. If you believe me now, why didn't you believe me a while ago when you asked if I'd seen Moorcroft?"

"Maggie, I did believe you," he reminded her patiently. "I asked you if you'd seen him before you left Seattle and you, with your usual straightforward style, told me you *had* seen Moorcroft, remember? You didn't deny it."

"But you didn't let me explain. You told me I had to answer yes or no."

"All right, I'm guilty of wanting a simple answer. I should have known that with you the explanation would be anything but simple. There are always complications around you, aren't there, Maggie? And you ran out the door without bothering to try to explain. What was I supposed to think?"

"That I would never have come down here for revenge," Maggie declared in ringing tones. "You should know me well enough to know that."

"Maggie, I know for a fact to what lengths a person will go for revenge. I also know how much I wanted you. It was entirely possible I'd deluded myself into thinking I'd really succeeded in convincing you to come back to me. God knows I want you back bad enough to tell myself all sorts of lies. But when you didn't deny the meeting with Moorcroft . . ."

"Never mind," Magaret said urgently. "Don't say it. I'm sorry. I should have stood my ground and yelled at you until you believed I was innocent."

Rafe's mouth curved gently. "You don't even have to yell. I'm always ready to listen."

"Hah. What a bunch of bull. You didn't listen last year."

"Yes, I did." Rafe sighed. "Maggie, last year you told me the truth, too. I listened to every damn word. When I caught you in Moorcroft's office you admitted immediately you'd just told him I was after Spencer, remember? You said you'd had to tell him—that it was your duty as a loyal employee of Moorcroft."

"Oh. Yes, I did say that, didn't I?"

"Our problem last year had nothing to do with your lying to me. You were too damned honest, if you want to know the truth. I'll tell you something. I would have sold my soul for a few sweet lies from you last year. More than anything else in this world I wanted to believe you hadn't felt your first loyalty was to Jack Moorcroft instead of me."

Margaret closed her eyes, feeling utterly wretched. "Are you ever going to be able to forgive me for that, Rafe? I don't know if we can go on together if you aren't able to understand why I did what I did."

"Hell, yes, I forgive you." Rafe pulled two more glasses out of his desk drawer and splashed Scotch into each. He handed one glass to Margaret who clutched it in both hands. "I hate to admit it, Maggie, love, but I was the idiot last year. You want to know something?"

"What?" she asked warily.

"I didn't think I'd ever say this, but I admire you for what you did. You were right. In that situation your business loyalties belonged to Moorcroft. You were his employee, drawing a salary from him and you believed you'd betrayed his interests by talking too freely to me. You did the right thing by going to him and telling him everything. I only wish I could count on all of my employees having a similar set of ethics."

Margaret couldn't believe what she was hearing. A surge of euphoric relief went through her. "Thank you, Rafe. That's very generous of you."

Rafe took a swallow of Scotch. "Mind you, I could have throttled you at the time and it took me months to calm down, but that doesn't change the facts. You did what you thought was right, even when the chips were down. You've got guts, Maggie."

She grinned slowly. "And out here in the Wild West you admire guts in a woman, right?"

"Hell, yes. No place for wimpy females around here."

"I thought you said I was soft. Too soft for the business world."

"That's different. You're a woman. Being soft doesn't mean you don't have guts."

Margaret got up, put her glass of Scotch down on the desk and walked around to sit on Rafe's knee. She put her arms around his neck and leaned her forehead down to rest against his. "You are a hopelessly chauvinistic, anachronistic, retrograde cowboy, but I love you, anyway."

"I know," he said, his voice dropping into the deep husky register that always sent shivers down Maggie's spine. "I've been fairly certain of it all along but I knew it for sure when you grabbed me by the shirt a minute ago, shoved me into this chair and begged me to listen to you."

"I did not exactly beg."

He smiled. "Pleaded?"

"Never. Well, maybe a little."

His smile widened into a grin. "It's okay, Maggie. I love you, too. More than anything else on God's earth. And just to prove how insightful, sensitive and intuitive I can be, I'll tell you that I understand what you went through a while ago when you came in here and pinned me down."

"You do?"

"Honey, I know first hand what it's like to stomp all over your own pride."

"Actually, it's not quite as bad an exercise as I thought it would be."

"I don't know about that. Personally I wouldn't want to have to repeat it too many times. Once was enough for me."

She relaxed against him. "What about Hatcher?"

Rafe tipped her head back against his shoulder and kissed her exposed throat. "Don't worry about him. There's no real harm done. I told you I've been letting him see bad information. The Ellington deal is safe."

"Yes, but, Rafe, don't you think you should try to understand why he did it?"

"I do understand. He's a yellow-bellied snake."

"But, Rafe . . ."

"I said, don't worry about it." He kissed her full on the mouth, a long, slow kiss that made her tremble in his arms. "That's better," Rafe said. "Now you're paying full attention."

He got up with her in his arms and carried her out of the study and down the hall to her bedroom.

A LONG WHILE LATER Margaret stirred amid the sheets, opened her eyes and blinked at the hot, lazy sunlight that dappled the patio outside the glass door. She knew without lifting her head to see his face that Rafe was wide awake. His arm was around her, holding her close against his side but his gaze was on the bright light bouncing off the pool water.

"You're thinking about Hatcher, aren't you?" Margaret asked.

"Yeah."

"What are you going to do, Rafe?"

"Fire him."

She didn't move. "And the Ellington deal?"

"It'll go through."

"This isn't just a case of beating Moorcroft to the punch, is it?"

"No."

"Rafe, tell me what you're planning. I have to know why this Ellington thing is so special to you."

"It doesn't concern you, Maggie, love. Let it be."

She sat up, holding the sheet to her breasts and searched his face. "It does concern me. I can feel it. Please tell me the truth, Rafe. I have to know what you're going to do."

He regarded her in silence for a long moment. "You won't like it, Maggie. You're too gentle to understand why I'm doing it."

"I've got guts, remember? *Tell me.*"

He shrugged in resignation. "All right, I'll spell it out. But don't say I didn't warn you. The Ellington deal is the first falling domino in a long line that's going to end with Moorcroft Industries."

Margaret froze. "What are you talking about?"

"I've lured Moorcroft way out on a limb. He's mortgaged to the hilt. Going after Ellington will weaken him still further. There's no way he'll be able to fend off a takeover when I get ready to do it."

"You're going to put him out of business? Destroy Moorcroft Industries?" Margaret was appalled. "Rafe, you can't do that."

"Watch me."

Horrified, Margaret grabbed his bare shoulder. "It's because of me, isn't it? You're going to ruin Jack Moorcroft because of what happened last year. He was right.

The business rivalry between the two of you has escalated into something else, something ugly."

"This is between Moorcroft and me. Don't concern yourself."

"Are you nuts? How can I help but concern myself? I'm the cause of this mess."

"No."

Margaret shook her head. "That's not true. Answer one question for me, Rafe. Would you be plotting now to take over Moorcroft Industries if that fiasco last year hadn't occurred?"

He eyed her consideringly. "No."

"So you're doing this on account of me."

"Maggie, love, don't get upset. I told you you wouldn't understand."

"I do understand. I understand only too well. You're bent on revenge. You have been all along."

"He's got to pay, Maggie. One way or another."

She could have cut herself on the sharp edges of his voice. "You can't blame him because I felt loyal to him. Rafe, that's not fair. I'm the one you should punish."

"It wasn't your fault you felt loyal to him," Rafe said impatiently. "I told you that. If it makes you feel any better, I don't blame Moorcroft, either. At least not for your sense of loyalty."

"Then why are you plotting to destroy him?" Margaret asked wildly.

"Because of the things he said and implied about you after you left his office that morning."

Margaret was truly shaken now. "Oh, my God. You mean that stuff about me having been his mistress? But, Rafe, he was lying."

"I know. I'm going to see he pays for the insults and the lies he told about you."

"You're doing all this to avenge my honor or something?" she gasped as it finally sank in.

"If you want to put it that way, yes. He shouldn't have said what he did about you, Maggie."

Dazed, Margaret got out of bed and picked up the nearest garment to cover herself. It was Rafe's shirt. She thrust her arms into the long sleeves, sat down on the edge of the bed and clasped her hands. The enormity of what he was planning in the name of vengeance nearly swamped her.

"Rafe, you can't do it," she finally whispered.

"Sure I can. Code of the West and all that, remember?"

"This is not funny. Don't try to make a joke out of it. Rafe, I can't have this on my conscience." She shook her head. "An entire company in ruins because of a few nasty remarks made by some male flaunting his latest victory. I can't bear to be the cause of so much destruction. I fully agree Moorcroft shouldn't have said those things to you."

"Damn right."

"Look, he was deliberately taunting you because he knew he'd won on the Spencer deal. You know how men are, always pushing, jostling, shouldering each other around. They see everything in terms of victory and defeat and when they see themselves as winners, they like to rub it in."

"Thank you for giving me the benefit of your deep, psychological insights into the male sex, ma'am. I think I like the Code of the West approach better, though. It's simpler."

"That's because you like to think in terms of black and white. Rafe, my father himself said that whole mess last year was one big area of gray and he's a great one for preferring things in black and white. If he can let it go, you can, too. We have each other now. That's all that really counts."

"Moorcroft has to pay, Maggie, and that's all there is to it. Stay out of it."

"I can't stay out of it. I caused it. You've said so yourself, often enough. Think about what you're doing. Granted Moorcroft was out of line in the things he said, but he doesn't deserve to be destroyed because of it. He's put his whole life into Moorcroft Industries, just as you've put yours into Cassidy and Company. Furthermore, there will be dozens of jobs on the line. You know that. These things always cost a lot of jobs. Innocent people will get hurt."

"For God's sake, don't try to make me feel sorry for the man or his company."

"Then try feeling sorry for me," she snapped. "I'm going to have to bear this burden on my conscience for the rest of my life."

"Hell. I was afraid you'd feel that way. I told you, you're too soft when it comes to things like this, Maggie. This is the way the business world functions and that's all there is to it."

"You mean this is the way men function."

"Amounts to the same thing. We still run the business world."

Margaret leaped to her feet in frustration. "I can't stand it. I have never met such a stubborn, thickheaded, unreasonable creature in my whole life. Rafe, you are being impossible. Utterly impossible."

"What the hell do you expect me to do? Act like that dim-witted Roarke Cody in *Ruthless* and let a multi-million-dollar deal go down the toilet just to please a woman?"

Margaret faced him from the foot of the bed, her hands on her hips. "Yes, damn it, that's exactly what I expect."

Rafe watched her with hooded eyes. "And if I don't agree to do what you want?"

"I will be furious."

"I don't care if you get mad. The question is, are you going to walk out on me?"

"No, I am not going to walk out on you, but I am going to be very, very angry and I will not hesitate to let you know it," she shouted.

"Prove it."

"Prove what? That I'm mad? What do you want me to do? Take a swing at you? Break a lamp over your head? Believe me, I'm tempted."

"No. Prove you won't walk out on me."

"The only way to prove it is to let you go through with this crazy revenge plan. And I won't agree to do that. I'm going to fight you every inch of the way, Rafe, I promise you."

Rafe laced his fingers behind his head and leaned back against the pillows. "You still don't understand. I want you to marry me. Now. Tonight. We can take a plane to Vegas."

Margaret took a step backward, shocked. "Marry you? Tonight? Why? What will that prove? You already know I love you. What's the rush?"

Rafe's smile was dangerous. "Maybe I still feel a little uncertain of you. Maybe I want to know you won't threaten to postpone the marriage as a means of manipulating me into doing what you want. Maybe I want to know that this time you love me enough to marry me even though you're madder than hell at me."

Margaret exploded. "You sneaky son of a... You weren't satisfied with the way I bloodied my knees in that little scene down the hall a while ago, were you? You want me to trample my pride right into the dust, don't you?"

Rafe shook his head. "No. I just want to know that you'll marry me even knowing you can't change me and that you aren't always going to like the way I operate."

Margaret threw up her hands in a gesture of exasperated surrender. "All right, I'll marry you."

"Now? Tonight?"

"If that's what you want. But I promise you I am going to argue this thing about crushing Moorcroft with you all the way to Vegas and back."

Rafe grinned. "It's a deal. Get dressed while I phone the airlines and see how soon we can get out of here."

11

Two days after his marriage, Rafe strode past two startled secretaries and straight into Moorcroft's office. Moorcroft looked up at the intrusion, his expression at first annoyed and then immediately cautious.

"Well, hello, Cassidy. What brings you to San Diego?"

Rafe tossed the Ellington file onto the desk in front of the other man. Then he removed his pearl gray Stetson and hung it on the end of the sleek Italian-style desk lamp.

"Unfinished business," Rafe explained, dropping into a black leather chair.

Moorcroft hesitated and then opened the file. He scanned the contents, absorbing the implications quickly. When he looked up again, his mouth was tight. "So you knew about my pipeline into your office all along? Knew Hatcher was keeping me informed?"

"I figured something was going on. He used to be a good man. One of the best. But he's changed recently."

"Probably because you've changed." Moorcroft leaned back in his chair. "And he didn't like the change."

"Is that right?" Rafe casually put his silver- and turquoise-trimmed boots on Hatcher's richly polished desk. "What didn't he like?"

Moorcroft sighed mockingly. "Don't you understand? You were his idol, Cassidy. The fastest gun in the

West. Hatcher thought he was working for the best and he liked being on the winning side. But during the past year he decided you'd lost your edge."

"No kidding."

"Afraid so. In his opinion you'd become obsessed with a certain woman and that obsession had weakened you. A young man on the way up does not like discovering his idol has an Achilles' heel. You were no longer the hotshot gunslinger he'd gone to work for three years ago. No longer the toughest, meanest, fastest desperado on the coast."

Rafe nodded. "I think I get the picture."

"Apparently for the past six months all you've done is plot revenge against me and worked on ways of getting Miss Lark back into your bed. Revenge he could understand, but not your single-minded desire to bed one specific lady."

"Looks like I failed as a role model."

"Something like that. It bothered him, Cassidy. When I contacted him on the off chance I could buy him, I discovered he was ripe for the picking."

"And you offered him a way to prove his newfound loyalty to you."

"What did you expect me to do?"

"Exactly what you did do, I suppose."

Moorcroft shrugged. "You'd have done the same. We live and die on the basis of inside information in this business, Cassidy. You know that. We take it where we can get it."

"True. Going to give him a job when he comes looking for one?"

"Hell, no. The guy's proven he's the type who will sell out his own boss. What do I want with him?"

"Figured you say that."

Moorcroft glanced at the Ellington file. "But in this case it looks like Hatcher may have been a little premature in writing you off. He's been feeding me false information almost from the start, hasn't he?"

"Yeah."

"And especially for the past week or so. It's too late for me to counter now, isn't it? Congratulations, Cassidy. Looks like you win this one." Moorcroft reached behind his chair and opened a small, discreet liquor cabinet. "You drink Scotch, according to Hatcher. Can I offer you a glass?"

"Sure."

Moorcroft poured Scotch into two glasses and pushed one across the desk to Rafe. Then he raised his own glass in a small salute. "Here's to the thrill of victory. I guess this makes us even, doesn't it? I got Spencer last year. You get Ellington this year."

"It's not quite that simple, Moorcroft. Check the printout at the end of that file."

Moorcroft hesitated and then reopened the Ellington file. He flipped to the last page and scanned the detailed financial forecast and spreadsheet he found there. Then he looked up again. "So?"

"So Ellington was merely the first."

"I can see that. Brisken was next?"

"And then Carlisle."

Moorcroft's eyes narrowed. "Carlisle? What do you want with it?"

"Guess."

Moorcroft slowly closed the file again. "Carlisle has a major stake in Moorcroft Industries at the moment. You take control of them and you have a chunk of me."

"You've got it."

Moorcroft swallowed the remainder of his Scotch in one long gulp. His fingers were very tight around the glass as he carefully set it down in front of him. "I was right, wasn't I?" he asked softly. "You are gunning for me."

"That was the plan," Rafe agreed. He studied the San Diego skyline outside the window. "Ellington, Brisken, Carlisle, and then Moorcroft. Dominoes all lined up in a neat little row."

"Why are you telling me this in advance? You're giving me time to maneuver. Why do that?"

"Because I'm canceling my plans. I've changed my mind. I'm not going to topple my little row of dominoes after all. I just wanted you to know what almost happened." Rafe's mouth curved faintly. "It's about the only satisfaction I'm going to get."

"To what do I owe this unexpected generosity of spirit?" Moorcroft looked more wary than ever.

"My wife. She didn't like being the reason for the collapse of an empire the size of yours. She's a soft little creature in some ways." Rafe grinned and took a sip of Scotch. "Plenty of spirit, though. Feisty as hell. You haven't been through anything until you've been through a wedding night with a bride who wants to lecture you on business ethics."

"We're talking about Margaret Lark, I take it? You've married her?" Moorcroft looked a little bewildered.

"Day before yesterday."

"Congratulations," Moorcroft said dryly. "You're a lucky man. I guess I am, too, if the reason you're calling off the revenge bit is on account of her. Looks like she saved my tail. So she was worried enough about me to make you change your whole battle plan. Interesting."

"Don't get too excited," Rafe advised. "It wasn't you she was concerned about. It was all the other innocent people who would go down with you. There's always a lot of bloodletting in the case of an unfriendly takeover. You know that."

"She wouldn't want that on her conscience."

"No."

"She's a real lady, isn't she?"

"Yeah. She's a lady all right. You forgot that last year."

Moorcroft nodded. "I shouldn't have said some of the things I did last year."

"No," Rafe agreed, his eyes still on the view.

"You know why I said them?"

"Sure. You wanted her and you knew you'd never have her," Rafe said succinctly.

"Never in a million years. She never gave me any sign of being interested in all the time she worked for me. Totally ignored every approach I tried to make. Then you appeared on the scene and she fell right into your hands."

"Yeah, well, if it makes you feel any better, I had something going for me you didn't have."

"What's that?" Moorcroft glanced in disgust at Rafe's hand-tooled boots.

"I was the man of her dreams. Straight out of one of her books."

"Women."

"Yeah." Rafe put his glass down on the desk and smiled fleetingly. "Maggie says they're going to take over the business world one of these days and show us how to run things right."

"I can't wait." Moorcroft looked at the Ellington file and then at Rafe. He frowned. "Is this business between us really over, Cassidy?"

"Almost." Rafe slid his boots off the desk, got up and peeled off his jacket. Then he started to roll up his sleeves.

"What the hell do you think you're doing?" Moorcroft got slowly to his feet.

"Finishing it." Rafe smiled. "You get to keep your company but I can't let you get off scot-free after insulting my wife's honor. One way or another you've got to pay for that, Moorcroft. You know how it is. Code of the West and all that."

"I suppose it won't do me any good to remind you she wasn't your wife at the time?"

"Nope. Doesn't matter. She still belonged to me. She has since the day I met her, whether she knew it or not. You want to take off your jacket so it doesn't get messed up? Looks like nice material."

Moorcroft eyed him for a long moment. Then he sighed again, shrugged off his jacket and unfastened the gold links on his cuffs.

Rafe went over to the door and locked it.

When he walked out of the office ten minutes later he paused briefly to tug his Stetson low over his eyes. He smiled brilliantly at the two secretaries. "Your boss won't be taking any more appointments today, ladies."

"YOU'RE MARRIED? What the hell do you mean, you're married?" Connor Lark roared at his daughter as he climbed out of the car and went around to the passenger side to open the door for Bev. "We go away for a few days to give you and Cassidy a chance to work out your differences and you up and get hitched. Couldn't you at least have waited until we got back?"

"Sorry, Dad, Rafe was in a hurry. Hello, Bev. How was Sedona?"

"Just lovely." Bev gave her a quick hug and then stood back to look at her new daughter-in-law. "Did that son of mine really marry you while we were gone?"

"It was real cheap and tacky, Bev. A Vegas wedding, no less. But it was for real." Margaret smiled warmly at the older woman but a part of her was waiting to make certain Bev approved. *You'd make him a better mistress than a wife.*

"My dear, I couldn't be more delighted," Bev said gently. "You'll make him a wonderful wife. And Rafe knew it all along. We'll have to give him credit for that, won't we? Don't worry about the cheap and tacky wedding. We'll make up for it with a lovely reception. I can't wait to start planning it."

"Well, there's no rush," Margaret assured her dryly. "The groom isn't even in town."

Connor plucked a suitcase out of the trunk. "Where the devil is he?"

"Took off this morning with hardly a goodbye kiss. Just announced at breakfast he was catching a plane to California. I haven't seen him since. Can you imagine? And after all those promises he made about not letting his business dominate his life anymore, he no sooner gets my name on a marriage certificate than he takes off. I guess the honeymoon is over."

Bev frowned. "Is that true, dear? He's gone off on business? I can't believe he'd do such a thing."

"I can." Margaret grinned. "But in this case I'm going to let him get away with it. I think I know where he went."

"Yeah?" Connor turned his head at the sound of a familiar car coming up the long, sweeping drive. "Where was that?"

Margaret watched the Mercedes come toward them, a sense of deep satisfaction welling up within her. "He had to take care of some unfinished business in San Diego."

The Mercedes came to a halt and Rafe got out. Margaret raced toward him and threw herself into his arms. "It's about time you got here," she whispered against his chest as she hugged him fiercely.

Rafe sucked in his breath and winced slightly. "Easy, honey."

Margaret looked up in alarm. "Rafe, are you all right?"

"Never better." He was grinning again as he bent his head to kiss her soundly.

"I was afraid you wouldn't get home this evening."

"Hey, I'm a married man now. I've got responsibilities here at home." He looked at Connor and Bev and nodded a friendly greeting. "Looks like we're going to be one big happy family again tonight. Damn. I was hoping for a little privacy. This is supposed to be a honeymoon, you know."

"Don't worry, Cassidy, your Mom and I won't be staying long," Connor assured him. "We're on our way to California. Just wanted to check up on you two and make sure you hadn't throttled each other while we were out of town."

"As you can see, Maggie and I have worked out our little differences. Hang on a second."

Rafe released Margaret to open the rear door of the Mercedes. He reached inside to remove a large, flat parcel.

"What's that?" Margaret asked curiously.

"A wedding present."

Margaret quickly dragged the package into the house and ripped off the protective wrapping while everyone stood around and watched. She laughed up at Rafe with sheer delight as she stood back to admire Sean Winters's *Canyon*.

"It's beautiful, Rafe. Thank you."

"I still think it looks like a bunch of squiggly lines but I'll try to think of it as an investment in my future brother-in-law's career."

MUCH LATER THAT NIGHT Margaret snuggled up beside her husband, drew an interesting circle on his bare chest and smiled in the shadows. "You went to see Jack Moorcroft today, didn't you?"

Rafe caught her teasing fingers and kissed them. "Uh-huh."

"You told him he was off the hook? That you aren't going to ruin him?"

"That's what I told him, all right."

Margaret levered herself up on her elbow to look down at him. "Rafe, I'm so proud of you for being able to handle that situation in a mature, reasonable, civilized fashion."

"That's me," he agreed, his lips on the inside of her wrist, "a mature, reasonable, civilized man."

Margaret studied his bent head and experienced a sudden jolt of unworthy suspicion. "You did behave in a mature, reasonable, civilized way when you went to see him, didn't you, Rafe?"

"Sure." He was kissing her shoulder now, pushing her gently back down onto the pillows.

"No Code of the West stuff or anything?" she persisted as she felt herself slipping under his sensual spell. "Rafe, you didn't do anything rash while you were visiting Moorcroft, did you?"

He kissed her throat and then raised his head to look down at her with gleaming eyes. "Maggie, love, I'm a businessman, not a gunfighter or an outlaw. Your romantic imagination sometimes gets a little carried away."

"I'm not so sure about that. Where you're concerned, my romantic imagination tends to be right on target." She reached up to put her arms around his neck and draw him down to her. "Remind me in the morning to send a telegram to some friends."

"Sure. Anything you say, Maggie, love. In the meantime what do you say we go for another midnight ride?"

"That sounds wonderful," she whispered, looking up at him with all her love in her eyes.

KATHERINE INSKIP HAWTHORNE got her telegram while she was eating papaya at breakfast with her husband on Amethyst Island. Sarah Fleetwood Trace found hers waiting for her when she got back from a treasure-hunting honeymoon.

Married a cowboy. Definitely an old-fashioned kind of guy. Code of the West, etc. A little rough around the edges but fantastic in the saddle. Can't wait for you to meet him. Suggest we all vacation on Amethyst Island this year.

Love,
Maggie

Sarah reached for the telephone at once and dialed Amethyst Island. "*Maggie?* She's let him talk her into letting herself be called Maggie?"

Katherine laughed on the other end of the line. "Obviously the woman is in love. How about that vacation here on the island?"

"Sounds like a truly brilliant idea to me," Sarah said, glancing at Gideon. "We'll all go treasure-hunting."

"It seems," said Katherine, "that we've already found our treasures."

"I think you're right."

HARLEQUIN
American Romance®

THE LOVES OF A CENTURY...

Join American Romance in a nostalgic look back at the Twentieth Century—at the lives and loves of American men and women from the turn-of-the-century to the dawn of the year 2000.

Journey through the decades from the dance halls of the 1900s to the discos of the seventies ... from Glenn Miller to the Beatles ... from Valentino to Newman ... from corset to miniskirt ... from beau to Significant Other.

Relive the moments ... recapture the memories.

Look now for the CENTURY OF AMERICAN ROMANCE series in Harlequin American Romance. In one of the four American Romance titles appearing each month, for the next twelve months, we'll take you back to a decade of the Twentieth Century, where you'll relive the years and rekindle the romance of days gone by.

Don't miss a day of the CENTURY OF AMERICAN ROMANCE.

A CENTURY OF
AMERICAN ROMANCE
1900's

The women...the men...the passions...
the memories....

CAR-1

Harlequin Superromance®

**A June title
not to be missed....**

Superromance author Judith Duncan has created her
most powerfully emotional novel yet, a book about
love too strong to forget and hate too painful to
remember....

Risen from the ashes of her past like a phoenix,
Sydney Foster knew too well the price of wisdom,
especially that gained in the underbelly of the city.
She'd sworn she'd never go back, but in order to
embrace a future with the man she loved, she had to
return to the streets...and settle an old score.

Once in a long while, you read a book that affects you
so strongly, you're never the same again. Harlequin is
proud to present such a book, STREETS OF FIRE by
Judith Duncan (Superromance #407). Her book merits
Harlequin's AWARD OF EXCELLENCE for June 1990,
conferred each month to one specially selected title.